L O V E

TONI MORRISON

LOVE

RANDOM HOUSE
LARGE PRINT

The Library of Congress has established a Cataloging-in-Publication record for this title

0–375–43233–7

www.randomlargeprint.com

FIRST LARGE PRINT EDITION

10 9 8 7 6 5 4 3 2 1

This Large Print edition published in accord with the standards of the N.A.V.H.

L O V E

The women's legs are spread wide open, so I hum. Men grow irritable, but they know it's all for them. They relax. Standing by, unable to do anything but watch, is a trial, but I don't say a word. My nature is a quiet one, anyway. As a child I was considered respectful; as a young woman I was called discreet. Later on I was thought to have the wisdom maturity brings. Nowadays silence is looked on as odd and most of my race has forgotten the beauty of meaning much by saying little. Now tongues work all by themselves with no help from the mind. Still, I used to be able to have normal conversations, and when the need arose, I could make a point strong enough to stop a womb—or a knife. Not anymore, because back in the seventies, when women began to straddle chairs and dance crotch out on television, when all the magazines started featuring behinds and inner thighs as though that's all there is to a woman, well, I shut up altogether. Before women agreed to spread in public, there used to be secrets—some to hold, some to tell. Now? No. Barefaced being the order of the day, I hum. The words dance in my head to the music in my mouth. People come in here for a plate of crawfish, or to pass the time, and never notice or care that they do all the talking. I'm background— the movie music that comes along when the sweethearts see each other for the first time, or when the husband is walking the beachfront alone wondering if anybody saw him doing the bad thing he couldn't help. My humming encourages people; frames their thoughts like when Mildred Pierce decides she has to go to jail for her daughter. I suspect, soft as it is, my music has that kind of influence too. The way "Mood Indigo" drifting across the waves can change the way you swim. It doesn't make you dive in, but it can set your stroke, or trick you into believing you are both smart and lucky. So why not swim farther and a little farther still? What's the deep to you? It's way down below, and has nothing to do with blood made bold by coronets and piano keys, does it? Of course, I don't claim that kind of power. My hum is mostly below range, private; suitable for an old woman embarrassed by the world; her way of objecting to how the century is turning out. Where all is known and nothing understood. Maybe it was always so, but it didn't strike me until some thirty years ago that prostitutes, looked up to for their honesty, have always set the style. Well, maybe it wasn't their honesty; maybe it was their success. Still, straddling a chair or dancing half naked on TV, these nineties women are not all that different from the respectable women who live around here. This is coast country, humid and God-fearing, where female recklessness runs too deep for short shorts or thongs or cameras. But then or now, decent underwear or none, wild women never could hide their innocence—a kind of pity-kitty hopefulness that their prince was on his way. Especially the tough ones with their box cutters and dirty language, or the glossy ones with two-seated cars and a pocketbook full of dope. Even the ones who wear scars like presidential medals and stockings rolled at their ankles can't hide the sugar-child, the winsome baby girl curled up somewhere inside, between the ribs, say, or under the heart. Naturally all of them have a sad story: too much notice, not enough, or the worst kind. Some tale about dragon daddies and false-hearted men, or mean mamas and friends who did them wrong. Each story has a monster in it who made them tough instead of brave, so they open their legs rather than their hearts where that folded child is tucked.

Sometimes the cut is so deep no woe-is-me tale is enough. Then the only thing that does the trick, that explains the craziness heaping up, holding down, and making women hate one another and ruin their children is an outside evil. People in Up Beach, where I'm from, used to tell about some creatures called Police-heads—dirty things with big hats who shoot up out of the ocean to harm loose women and eat disobedient children. My mother knew them when she was a girl and people dreamed wide awake. They disappeared for a while but came back with new and bigger hats starting in the forties when a couple of "See there, what'd I tell you?" things happened at the shore. Like that woman who furrowed in the sand with her neighbor's husband and the very next day suffered a stroke at the cannery, the grappling knife still in her hand. She wasn't but twenty-nine at the time. Another woman—she lived over in Silk and wouldn't have anything to do with Up Beach people—well, she hid a flashlight and a purchase deed in the sand of her father-in-law's beachfront one evening only to have a loggerhead dig them up in the night. The miserable daughter-in-law broke her wrist trying to keep the breezes and the Klan away from the papers she'd stolen. Of course nobody flat out saw any Police-heads during the shame of those guilty women, but I knew they were around and knew what they looked like, too, because I'd already seen them in 1942 when some hard-headed children swam past the safety rope and drowned. As soon as they were pulled under, thunderclouds gathered above a screaming mother and a few dumbstruck picnickers and, in a blink, those clouds turned into gate-mouthed profiles wearing wide-brimmed hats. Some folks heard rumbling but I swear I heard whoops of joy. From that time on through the fifties they loitered above the surf or hovered over the beach ready to pounce around sunset (you know, when lust is keenest, when loggerheads hunt nests and negligent parents get drowsy). Of course most demons get hungry at suppertime, like us. But Police-heads liked to troll at night, too, especially when the hotel was full of visitors drunk with dance music, or salt air, or tempted by starlit water. Those were the days when Cosey's Hotel and Resort was the best and best-known vacation spot for colored folk on the East Coast. Everybody came: Lil Green, Fatha Hines, T-Bone Walker, Jimmy Lunceford, the Drops of Joy, and guests from as far away as Michigan and New York couldn't wait to get down here. Sooker Bay swirled with first lieutenants and brand-new mothers; with young schoolteachers, landlords, doctors, businessmen. All over the place children rode their fathers' leg shanks and buried uncles up to their necks in sand. Men and women played croquet and got up baseball teams whose goal was to knock a homer into the waves. Grandmothers watched over red thermos jugs with white handles and hampers full of crabmeat salad, ham, chicken, yeast rolls, and loaves of lemon-flavored cake, oh my. Then, all of a sudden, in 1958, bold as a posse, the Police-heads showed up in bright morning. A clarinet player and his bride drowned before breakfast. The inner tube they were floating on washed ashore dragging wads of scale-cluttered beard hair. Whether the bride had played around during the honeymoon was considered and whispered about, but the facts were muddy. She sure had every opportunity. Cosey's Resort had more handsome single men per square foot than anyplace outside Atlanta or even Chicago. They came partly for the music but mostly to dance by the sea with pretty women.

After the drowned couple was separated—sent to different funeral parlors—you'd think women up to no good and mule-headed children wouldn't need further warning, because they knew there was no escape: fast as lightning, nighttime or day, Police-heads could blast up out of the waves to punish way-ward women or swallow the misbehaving young. Only when the resort failed did they sneak off like pickpockets from a breadline. A few people still sink-ing crab castles in the back bays probably remember them, but with no more big bands or honeymooners, with the boats and picnics and swimmers gone, when Sooker Bay became a treasury of sea junk and Up Beach itself drowned, nobody needed or wanted to recall big hats and scaly beards. But it's forty years on, now; the Coseys have disappeared from public view and I'm afraid for them almost every day.

Except for me and a few fish shacks, Up Beach is twenty feet underwater; but the hotel part of Cosey's Resort is still standing. Sort of standing. Looks more like it's rearing backwards—away from hurricanes and a steady blow of sand. Odd what oceanfront can do to empty buildings. You can find the prettiest shells right up on the steps, like scattered petals or cameos from a Sunday dress, and you wonder how they got there, so far from the ocean. Hills of sand piling in porch corners and between banister railings are whiter than the beach, and smoother, like twice-sifted flour. Foxglove grows waist high around the gazebo, and roses, which all the time hate our soil, rage here, with more thorns than blackberries and weeks of beet red blossoms. The wood siding of the hotel looks silver-plated, its peeling paint like the streaks on an unpolished tea service. The big double doors are padlocked. So far nobody has smashed their glass panels. Nobody could stand to do it because the panels mirror your own face as well as the view behind your back: acres of chive grass edging the sparkly beach, a movie-screen sky, and an ocean that wants you more than anything. No matter the outside loneliness, if you look inside, the hotel seems to promise you ecstasy and the company of all your best friends. And music. The shift of a shutter hinge sounds like the cough of a trumpet; piano keys waver a quarter note above the wind so you might miss the hurt jamming those halls and closed-up rooms.

Our weather is soft, mostly, with peculiar light. Pale mornings fade into white noons, then by three o'clock the colors are savage enough to scare you. Jade and sapphire waves fight each other, kicking up enough foam to wash sheets in. An evening sky behaves as though it's from some other planet—one without rules, where the sun can be plum purple if it wants to and clouds can be red as poppies. Our shore is like sugar, which is what the Spaniards thought of when they first saw it. Sucra, they called it, a name local whites tore up for all time into Sooker.

Nobody could get enough of our weather except when the cannery smell got to the beach and into the hotel. Then guests discovered what Up Beach people put up with every day and thought that was why Mr. Cosey moved his family out of the hotel and built that big house on Monarch Street. Fish odor didn't used to be all that bad a thing in these parts. Like marsh stench and privies, it just added another variety to the senses. But in the sixties it became a problem. A new generation of females complained about what it did to their dresses, their appetite, and their idea of romance. This was around the time the world decided perfume was the only smell the nose was meant for. I remember Vida trying to calm the girlfriend of a famous singer who was carrying on about her steak tasting like conch. That hurt me, because I have never failed in the kitchen. Later on, Mr. Cosey told people that's what ruined his busi-

ness—that the whites had tricked him, let him buy all the oceanfront he wanted because the cannery, so close by, kept it unprofitable. The fish smell had turned his resort into a joke. But I know that the smell that blanketed Up Beach hit Sooker Bay only once or twice a month—and never from December to April, when crab castles were empty and the cannery closed. No. I don't care what he told people, something else wrecked his resort. Freedom, May said. She tried hard to keep the place going when her father-in-law lost interest, and was convinced that civil rights destroyed her family and its business. By which she meant colored people were more interested in blowing up cities than dancing by the seashore. She was like that, May; but what started out as mule-headed turned into crack-brained. Fact is, folks who bragged about Cosey vacations in the forties boasted in the sixties about Hyatts, Hiltons, cruises to the Bahamas and Ocho Rios. Truth is, neither shellfish nor integration was to blame. Never mind the woman with the conch-flavored steak, customers will sit next to a privy if it's the only way they can hear Wilson Pickett or Nellie Lutcher. Besides, who can tell one odor from another while pressed close to a partner on a crowded dance floor listening to "Harbor Lights"? And while May kept blaming Martin Luther King every day for her troubles, the hotel still made money, although with a different clientele. Listen to me: something else was to blame.

Besides, Mr. Cosey was a smart man. He helped more colored people here than forty years of government programs. And he wasn't the one who boarded up the hotel and sold seventy-five acres to an Equal Opportunity developer for thirty-two houses built so cheap my shack puts them to shame. At least my floors are hand-planed oak, not some slicked-up pine, and if my beams aren't ruler smooth, they're true and properly aged when hoisted.

Before Up Beach drowned in a hurricane called Agnes, there was a drought with no name at all. The sale had just closed, the acres barely plotted, when Up Beach mothers were pumping mud from their spigots. Dried-up wells and brackey water scared them so, they gave up the sight of the sea and applied for a two-percent HUD mortgage. Rainwater wasn't good enough for them anymore. Trouble, unemployment, hurricanes following droughts, marshland turned into mud cakes so dry even the mosquitoes quit—I saw all that as life simply being itself. Then the government houses went up and they named the neighborhood Oceanside—which it isn't. The developers started out selling to Vietnam veterans and retired whites, but when Oceanside became a target for people thrown out of work onto food stamps, churches and this affirmative action stuff got busy. Welfare helped some till urban renewal came to town. Then there were jobs all over the place. Now, it's full of people commuting to offices and hos-

pital labs twenty-two miles north. Traveling back and forth from those cheap, pretty houses to malls and movieplexes, they're so happy they haven't had a cloudy thought, let alone a memory of Police-heads. They didn't cross my mind either until I started to miss the Cosey women and wonder if they'd finally killed each other. Who besides me would know if they were dead in there—one vomiting on the steps still holding the knife that cut the throat of the one that fed her the poison? Or if one had a stroke after shooting the other and, not able to move, starved to death right in front of the refrigerator? They wouldn't be found for days. Not until Sandler's boy needed his weekly pay. Maybe I best leave off the TV for a while.

I used to see one of them driving along in that rusty old Oldsmobile—to the bank or in here, once in a while, for Salisbury steak. Otherwise they haven't left that house in years. Not since one came back carrying a Wal-Mart shopping bag and you could tell by the set of her shoulders she was whipped. The white Samsonite luggage she left with was nowhere in sight. I thought the other one would slam the door in her face, but she didn't. I guess they both knew they deserved each other. Meaner than most and standoffish, they have the regular attention that disliked folks attract. They live like queens in Mr. Cosey's house, but since that girl moved in there a while ago with a skirt short as underpants and no *underpants at all, I've been worried about them leaving me here with nothing but an old folks' tale to draw on. I know it's trash: just another story made up to scare wicked females and correct unruly children. But it's all I have. I know I need something else. Something better. Like a story that shows how brazen women can take a good man down. I can hum to that.*

I

———————————————————

PORTRAIT

The day she walked the streets of Silk, a chafing wind kept the temperature low and the sun was helpless to move outdoor thermometers more than a few degrees above freezing. Tiles of ice had formed at the shoreline and, inland, the thrown-together houses on Monarch Street whined like puppies. Ice slick gleamed, then disappeared in the early evening shadow, causing the sidewalks she marched along to undermine even an agile tread, let alone one with a faint limp. She should have bent her head and closed her eyes to slits in that weather, but being a stranger, she stared wide-eyed at each house, searching for the address that matched the one in the advertisement: One Monarch Street. Finally she turned into a driveway where Sandler Gibbons stood in his garage door ripping the seam from a sack of Ice-Off. He remembers the crack of her heels on concrete as she approached; the angle of her hip as she stood there, the melon sun behind her, the garage light in her face. He remembers the pleasure of her voice when she asked for directions to the house of women he has known all his life.

"You sure?" he asked when she told him the address.

She took a square of paper from a jacket pocket, held it with ungloved fingers while she checked, then nodded.

Sandler Gibbons scanned her legs and reckoned her knees and thighs were stinging from the cold her tiny skirt exposed them to. Then he marveled at the height of her bootheels, the cut of her short leather jacket. At first he'd thought she wore a hat, something big and fluffy to keep her ears and neck warm. Then he realized that it was hair—blown forward by the wind, distracting him from her face. She looked to him like a sweet child, fine-boned, gently raised but lost.

"Cosey women," he said. "That's their place you looking for. It ain't been number one for a long time now, but you can't tell them that.

Can't tell them nothing. It 1410 or 1401, probably."

Now it was her turn to question his certainty.

"I'm telling you," he said, suddenly irritable—the wind, he thought, tearing his eyes. "Go on up thataway. You can't miss it 'less you try to. Big as a church."

She thanked him but did not turn around when he hollered at her back, "Or a jailhouse."

Sandler Gibbons didn't know what made him say that. He believed his wife was on his mind. She would be off the bus by now, stepping carefully on slippery pavement until she got to their driveway. There she would be safe from falling because, with the forethought and common sense he was known for, he was prepared for freezing weather in a neighborhood that had no history of it. But the "jailhouse" comment meant he was really thinking of Romen, his grandson, who should have been home from school an hour and a half ago. Fourteen, way too tall, and getting muscled, there was a skulk about him, something furtive that made Sandler Gibbons stroke his thumb every time the boy came into view. He and Vida Gibbons had been pleased to have him, raise him, when their daughter and son-in-law enlisted. Mother in the army; father in the merchant marines. The best choice out of none when only pickup work (housecleaning in Harbor for the women, hauling road trash for the men) was left after the cannery closed. "Parents idle, children sidle," his own mother used to say. Getting regular yard work helped, but not enough to keep Romen on the dime and out of the sight line of ambitious, under-occupied police. His own boyhood had been shaped by fear of vigilantes, but dark blue uniforms had taken over posse work now. What thirty years ago was a one-sheriff, one-secretary department was now four patrol cars and eight officers with walkie-talkies to keep the peace.

He was wiping salt dust from his hands when the two people under his care arrived at the same time, one hollering, "Hoo! Am I glad you did this! Thought I'd break my neck." The other saying, "What you mean, Gran? I had your arm all the way from the bus."

"Course you did, baby." Vida Gibbons smiled, hoping to derail any criticism her husband might be gathering against her grandson.

At dinner, the scalloped potatoes having warmed his mood, Sandler picked up the gossip he'd begun while the three of them were setting the table.

"What did you say she wanted?" Vida asked, frowning. The ham slices had toughened with reheating.

"Looking for those Cosey women, I reckon. That was the address she had. The old address, I mean. When wasn't nobody out here but them."

"That was written on her paper?" She poured a little raisin sauce over her meat.

"I didn't look at it, woman. I just saw her check it. Little scrap of something looked like it came from a newspaper."

"You were concentrating on her legs, I guess. Lot of information there."

Romen covered his mouth and closed his eyes.

"Vida, don't belittle me in front of the boy."

"Well, the first thing you told me was about her skirt. I'm just following your list of priorities."

"I said it was short, that's all."

"How short?" Vida winked at Romen.

"They wear them up to here, Gran." Romen's hand disappeared under the table.

"Up to where?" Vida leaned sideways.

"Will you two quit? I'm trying to tell you something."

"You think she's a niece, maybe?" asked Vida.

"Could be. Didn't look like one, though. Except for size, looked more like Christine's people." Sandler motioned for the jar of jalapeños.

"Christine don't have any people left."

"Maybe she had a daughter you don't know about." Romen just wanted to be in the conversation, but as usual, they looked at him as if his fly was open.

"Watch your mouth," said his grandfather.

"I'm just talking, Gramp. How would I know?"

"You wouldn't, so don't butt in."

"Stch."

"You sucking your teeth at me?"

"Sandler, lighten up. Can't you leave him alone for a minute?" Vida asked.

Sandler opened his mouth to defend his position, but decided to bite the tip off the pepper instead.

"Anyway, the less I hear about those Cosey girls, the better I like it," said Vida.

"Girls?" Romen made a face.

"Well, that's how I think of them. Hincty, snotty girls with as much cause to look down on people as a pot looks down on a skillet."

"They're cool with me," said Romen. "The skinny one, anyway."

Vida glared at him. "Don't you believe it.

She pays you; that's all you need from either one."

Romen swallowed. Now she was on his back. "Why you all make me work there if they that bad?"

"Make you?" Sandler scratched a thumb.

"Well, you know, send me over there."

"Drown this boy, Vida. He don't know a favor from a fart."

"We sent you because you need some kind of job, Romen. You've been here four months and it's time you took on some of the weight."

Romen tried to get the conversation back to his employers' weaknesses and away from his own. "Miss Christine always gives me something good to eat."

"I don't want you eating off her stove."

"Vida."

"I don't."

"That's just rumor."

"A rumor with mighty big feet. And I don't trust that other one either. I *know* what she's capable of."

"Vida."

"You forgot?" Vida's eyebrows lifted in surprise.

"Nobody knows for sure."

"Knows what?" asked Romen.

"Some old mess," said his grandfather.

Vida stood and moved to the refrigerator. "Somebody killed him as sure as I'm sitting here. Wasn't a thing wrong with that man." Dessert was canned pineapple in sherbet glasses. Vida set one at each place. Sandler, unimpressed, leaned back. Vida caught his look but decided to let it lie. She worked; he was on a security guard's hilarious pension. And although he kept the house just fine, she was expected to come home and cook a perfect meal every day.

"What man?" Romen asked.

"Bill Cosey," replied Sandler. "Used to own a hotel and a lot of other property, including the ground under this house."

Vida shook her head. "I saw him the day he died. Hale at breakfast; dead at lunch."

"He had a lot to answer for, Vida."

"Somebody answered for him: 'No lunch.' "

"You forgive that old reprobate anything."

"He paid us good money, Sandler, and taught us, too. Things I never would have known about if I'd kept on living over a swamp in a stilt house. You know what my mother's hands looked like. Because of Bill Cosey, none of us had to keep doing that kind of work."

"It wasn't that bad. I miss it sometimes."

"Miss what? Slop jars? Snakes?"

"The trees."

"Oh, shoot." Vida tossed her spoon into the sherbet glass hard enough to get the clink she wanted.

"Remember the summer storms?" Sandler ignored her. "The air just before—"

"Get up, Romen." Vida tapped the boy's shoulder. "Help me with the dishes."

"I ain't finished, Gran."

"Yes you are. Up."

Romen, forcing air through his lips, pushed back his chair and unfolded himself. He tried to exchange looks with his grandfather, but the old man's eyes were inward.

"Never seen moonlight like that anywhere else." Sandler's voice was low. "Make you want to—" He collected himself. "I'm not saying I would move back."

"I sure hope not." Vida scraped the plates loudly. "You'd need gills."

"Mrs. Cosey said it was a paradise." Romen reached for a cube of pineapple with his fingers.

Vida slapped his hand. "It was a plantation. And Bill Cosey took us off of it."

"The ones he wanted." Sandler spoke to his shoulder.

"I heard that. What's that supposed to mean?"

"Nothing, Vida. Like you said, the man was a saint."

"There's no arguing with you."

Romen dribbled liquid soap into hot water. His hands felt good sloshing in it, though it stung the bruises on his knuckles. His side hurt more while he stood at the sink, but he felt better listening to his grandparents fussing about the olden days. Less afraid.

The girl did not miss the house, and the man with the Ice-Off was not wrong: the house was graceful, imposing, and its peaked third-story roof did suggest a church. The steps to the porch, slanted and shiny with ice, encouraged caution, for there was no railing. But the girl clicked along the walk and up the steps without hesitation. Seeing no bell, she started to knock, hesitating when she noticed a shaft of light below, to the right of the porch. She went back down the sloping steps, followed the curve marked by half-buried slate, and descended a flight of iron stairs lit by a window. Beyond the window, a door. No wind buffeted her there. The area had the look of what was called a garden apartment by some— by others, a basement one. Pausing at the pane, she saw a seated woman. On the table before her were a colander, newspapers, and a mixing bowl. The girl tapped on the window and smiled when the woman looked up. She rose slowly but once on her feet moved rapidly to the door.

"What is it?" The door opened just wide enough to expose one gray eye.

"I came about the job," said the girl. A marine odor hovered in the crack.

"Then you're lost," said the woman and slammed the door.

The girl banged on it, shouting, "It says One Monarch Street! This is number one!"

There was no answer, so she went back to the window and pecked the glass with the nails of her left hand while her right pressed the newsprint toward the light.

The woman came back to the window, her eyes flat with annoyance as they stared at the girl, then moved from the young face and its pleading smile to the piece of paper. She squinted at it, looked again at the face, then back at the piece of paper. She motioned toward the door and disappeared from the window, but not before a shard of panic glinted in her eyes, then died.

When the girl was inside, the woman offered neither seat nor greeting. She took the advertisement and read. A penciled circle separated the few lines of one help-wanted notice from others above and below.

COMPANION, SECRETARY SOUGHT BY MATURE, PROFESSIONAL LADY. LIGHT BUT HIGHLY CONFIDENTIAL WORK. APPLY TO MRS. H. COSEY. ONE MONARCH STREET, SILK.

"Where did you get this?" The woman's tone was accusatory.

"From the newspaper."

"I can see that. Which? The *Harbor Journal*?"

"Yes, ma'am."

"When?"

"Today."

She handed back the advertisement. "Well. I guess you better sit down." The snap in her voice loosened.

"Are you Mrs. H. Cosey?"

She gave the girl a look. "If I was, I'd know about that little scrap of paper, wouldn't I?"

The girl's laughter was like the abrupt agitation of bells. "Oh, right. Sorry."

They both sat then and the woman returned to the work of deveining shrimp. Twelve rings, two on three fingers of each hand, snatched light from the ceiling fixture and seemed to elevate her task from drudgery to sorcery.

"You have a name?"

"Yes, ma'am. Junior."

The woman looked up. "Your daddy's idea?"

"Yes, ma'am."

"Have mercy."

"You can call me June, if you want."

"I don't want. Your daddy give you a last name? Prom, maybe? Or Choir?"

"Viviane," said Junior. "With an *e*."

"An *e*? You from around here?"

"Used to be. I've been away."

"I never heard tell of any family around here named Viviane with an *e* or without one."

"Oh, they're not from here. Originally."

"Where then?"

Jacket leather purred as Junior Viviane shrugged her shoulders and reached across the table to the colander. "Up north. Can I help you with that, ma'am?" she asked. "I'm a pretty fair cook."

"Don't." The woman held up a staying hand. "Needs a certain rhythm."

A bouquet of steam wandered away from water lifting to a boil on the stove. Behind the table was a wall of cupboards, their surfaces as pale and handled as yeast dough. The silence stretching between the two women tightened. Junior Viviane fidgeted, her jacket creaking over the tick of shrimp shells.

"Is Mrs. H. Cosey here, ma'am?"

"She is."

"May I speak to her, please?"

"Let me see that thing again." The woman wiped her hands on a dish towel before touching the ad. " 'Highly confidential,' huh?" She pursed her lips. "I believe that. I sure do," she said, and dropped the paper with thumb and forefinger, as though depositing a diaper into a soak pail. She wiped her hands again and selected a shrimp. There, just there, beneath the flesh she held in her fingers, crept a dark and tender line. Deft as a jeweler, she removed it.

"Can I see Mrs. Cosey now, please?" Junior sank her chin into her palm, underscoring her question with a smile.

"I guess. Sure. Up those stairs, then some more stairs. All the way to the top." She motioned toward a flight of stairs leading from an alcove near the stove. Junior stood.

"I don't suppose you interested in my name?"

Junior turned back, her grin a study in embarrassment and muddle. "Oh, yes, ma'am. I'm sorry. I am. I'm just so nervous."

"It's Christine. If you get the 'highly confidential' job you'll need to know it."

"I hope so. Nice meeting you, Christine. Really. Second floor, you said?"

Her boots were muffled on the stairs.

Christine turned away. She should have said, "No. Third," but she didn't. Instead she glanced at the warming light on the rice cooker. Gathering the shrimp shells, she plopped them into the boiling water and adjusted the flame. Returning to the table, she picked up a garlic paw and, enjoying her bedizened hands as usual, peeled two of the cloves. These she diced and left on the cutting board. The old Philco refrigerator murmured and trembled. Christine gave it a reassuring pat before bending to a low cabinet, thinking, What's she up to now? Must be scared or fixing to make a move. What, though? And how did she manage to get a notice in the paper without my knowing? She selected a silver tureen with a fitted glass bowl, sighing at the stubborn tarnish in the crevices of the *C*'s on its cover. Like all the carved letters in the house, the double *C*'s went beyond ornate to illegible. Even on the handle of the spoon in her apron pocket, the initials, once hooked together for life, were hardly a trace. It was tiny, a coffee spoon, but Christine ate every meal she could with it just to hold close the child it was given to, and hold also the pictures it summoned. Scooping peach slices with it from homemade ice cream, helpless in the thrill, never minding the grains of sand blowing over the dessert—the whole picnic lunch for that matter.

Christine soaped and rinsed the glass bowl as her thoughts skittered from beach picnics to Silver Dip, salt-spiced air to Q-tips, and on to the interview being held at that moment in the bedroom of the meanest woman on the coast. While sitting across from the lying Miss Junior-but-you-can-call-me-June, Christine had put her own body of forty—even thirty—years ago next to the girl's and won. The girl had good legs (well, knees and thighs were all she could see in those tall boots) and the narrow, poked-out behind that was all the rage these days. But she had nothing to rival the Christine of 1947, when the beach was the color of cream but glittery and the sucking waves reached out from water so blue you had to turn away lest it hurt your eyes. It was the girl's face that struck gongs of envy. That and her Amazon hair. At first Christine had stared at her, then, wary, concentrated on the newspaper clipping. Except for that, she would never have let into the house a strange girl with no purse. The shrimp work gave her ample time to get a bounce from her, some sense of what (never mind who) she was. It also gave her reason to sustain a lowered gaze, because she did not like the heart jump that came when she looked in the girl's eyes. She had the unnerving look of an underfed child. One you wanted to cuddle or slap for being needy.

Christine stirred the garlic into butter softening in a skillet, then set about making the roux. After a moment she sprinkled in flour and watched it bronze before loosening the paste with stock and whisking it smooth.

"I'm a pretty fair cook" is what the girl had said, all the while reaching with dirty hands for the bowl of cleaned shrimp. And "Used to be" from around here, she'd said, while sitting in front of the best-known woman in the county, a woman who knew every black person ever born from Niggerhead Rock to Sooker Bay, from Up Beach to Silk, and half the ones in Harbor as well, since that was where she had spent (or wasted) a whole chunk of her life. Junior Viviane. With an *e*. Sounded like a name from a baseball card. So what was the heart skip for? Was she afraid she would blush in recognition at any moment, sharpening her voice to a razor to cut off the possibility? The telltale signs of a runaway's street life were too familiar: bus station soap, other people's sandwiches, unwashed hair, slept-in clothes, no purse, mouth cleaned with chewing gum instead of toothpaste. So what did Heed want her for? How had an ad been placed in the newspaper without a working telephone? The Gibbons boy must have helped her—adding that errand to others after working in the yard. Whatever was going on was a trap laid by a high-heeled snake. Some new way to rob her future just as she had ripped off her past.

"I'll be damned," she whispered.

Christine spread her fingers for the familiar jolt the diamonds gave her. Then she assembled the rice, the shrimp, the sauce, layering each meticulously, artfully, in the casserole. It would remain warm while she tossed a light salad. Then she would arrange it all on a silver tray, take it up three flights of stairs, where she hoped it would choke the meanest thing on the coast.

"My Lord. Snow." She spoke without turning her head, simply parting the draperies further. "Come over here and look. Here of all places."

Junior moved near the tiny woman at the window and peered through the glass, trying but unable to see snowflakes. The woman looked to be in her sixties at least—hair made megablack by a thick border of silver at the scalp—but she had something of a little-girl scent: butter-rum candy, grass juice, and fur.

"Strange, don't you think? We never get snow. Never."

"I saw a man sprinkling ice salt," said Junior. "Since he already had it, he must have expected to use it."

Startled, the woman turned. The girl had called her a liar before saying hello.

"You're here for the job?" Her eyes swept Junior's face, then examined her clothes. She knew the applicant was in the house long before she heard footsteps that were neither Christine's nor Romen's. Then she had quickly positioned herself at the window to strike the right pose, give a certain impression. But she needn't have bothered. The girl was not at all what she had expected. Not just the messy hair and tacky clothes; there was some bold laziness in her manner, the way she talked. Like the "Yeah" she gave to Heed's question.

"Don't you mean 'Yes'?"

Like the kitchen below, this room was over-bright, like a department store. Every lamp— six? ten?—was on, rivaling the chandelier.

Mounting the unlit stairs, glancing over her shoulder, Junior had to guess what the other rooms might hold. It seemed to her that each woman lived in a spotlight separated—or connected—by the darkness between them. Staring openly at the items crowding the surfaces of tables, desks, she waited for the little woman to break the silence.

"I'm Heed Cosey. And you are?"

"Junior. But you can call me June."

"Oh, dear," said Heed, and batted her lashes as if someone had spilled red wine on pale velvet: sorry, of course, and no fault, of course, but difficult to clean nonetheless. Moving away from the window, she had to step carefully, so full was the room with furniture. A chaise, two dressers, two writing tables, side tables, chairs high-backed and low-seated. All under the influence of a bed behind which a man's portrait loomed. Heed sat down finally at a small desk. Placing her hands in her lap, she nodded for the girl to take the facing chair.

"Tell me where you have worked before. The notice didn't specify a resume, but I need to know your work history."

Junior smiled. The woman pronounced "resume" with two syllables. "I'm eighteen and can do anything you want. Anything."

"That's good to know, but references? Do

you have any? Someone I can get in touch with?"

"Nope."

"Well how will I know you are honest? Discreet?"

"A letter won't tell you even if it says so. I say I am. Hire me and you'll see. If I'm not good enough—" Junior turned her palms up.

Heed touched the corners of her lips with a hand small as a child's and crooked as a wing. She considered her instant dislike of the Junior-but-you-can-call-me-June person slouching in front of her and thought that her blunt speech, while not a pose, was something of an act. She considered something else too: whether the girl's attitude had staying power. She needed someone who could be coaxed into things or who already had a certain hunger. The situation was becoming urgent. Christine, true to her whore's heart, sporting diamonds in their rightful owner's face, was pilfering house money to pay a lawyer.

"Let me tell you what this job calls for. The duties, I mean."

"Go ahead." Junior shouldered out of her jacket, the cheap leather mewing. Under it, her black T-shirt gave no support to her breasts, but it was clear to Heed that they didn't need any: the nipples were high, martial. With the jacket off, her hair seemed to spring into view. Layers of corkscrews, parted in the middle, glinted jet in the lamplight.

"I'm writing a book," said Heed, a smile of satisfaction lighting her face. The posture she'd assumed to manage the interview changed with the mention of her book. "It's about my family. The Coseys. My husband's family."

Junior looked at the portrait. "That him?"

"That's him. It was painted from a snapshot, so it's exactly like him. What you see there is a wonderful man." Heed sighed. "Now I got all the material, but some things need checking, you know. Dates, spellings. I got each guest book from our hotel—except for two or three, I think—and some of those people, not many but some, had the worse handwriting. The worse. But most folks I seen had perfect hands, you know, because that's the way we was taught. But Papa didn't let them print it the way they do now, right alongside the signature. Didn't need to anyway, because he knowed everybody who was anybody and could recognize a signature even if it was a X, but no X-type people came, of course. Our guests, most of them, had gorgeous handwriting because, between you and I, you had to be more than just literate, you had to have a position, an accomplishment, understand? You couldn't achieve nothing worthwhile if your handwriting was low. Nowadays people write with they feet."

Heed laughed, then said, "Excuse me. You have no idea, do you, what I'm talking about. I get excited is all, just thinking about it." She adjusted the lapels of her housecoat with her thumbs, readdressing herself to the interview. "But I want to hear about you. 'Junior,' you said?"

"Yeah."

"Well now, Junior. You said you can do anything I want, so you must have worked somewhere before. If you're going to help me with my book I need to know—"

"Look, Mrs. Cosey. I can read; I can write, okay? I'm as smart as it gets. You want handwriting, you want typing, I'll do it. You want your hair fixed, I'll fix it. You want a bath, I'll give you one. I need a job and I need a place to stay. I'm real good, Mrs. Cosey. Really real good." She winked, startling Heed into a momentary recall of something just out of reach, like a shell snatched away by a wave. It may have been that flick of melancholy so sharply felt that made her lean close to the girl and whisper,

"Can you keep a secret?" She held her breath.

"Like nobody you ever knew."

Heed exhaled. "Because the work is private. Nobody can know about it. Not nobody."

"You mean Christine?"

"I mean nobody."

"I'll take it."

"You don't even know what the pay is."

"I'll take the job. You'll pay. Should I start now or wait till tomorrow?"

Footsteps, slow and rhythmic, sounded in the hall.

"Tomorrow," Heed said. She whispered the word, but it had the urgency of a shout.

Christine entered carrying a tray. No knock preceded her and no word accompanied her. She placed the tray on the desk where Heed and Junior faced each other and left without meeting a single eye.

Heed lifted the casserole lid, then replaced it. "Anything to annoy me," she said.

"Looks delicious," said Junior.

"Then you eat it," said Heed.

Junior forked a shrimp into her mouth and moaned, "Mmmm, God, she sure knows how to cook."

"What she knows is, I don't eat shellfish."

The second floor had none of the fussy comfort Junior found on the third. Here a hallway, two plain bedrooms, a kind of office, and a bathroom equaled the entire square footage of the room above, where Junior had spent two hours trying to read the woman who was now her boss.

It should not have taken that long but the taste of hot, home-cooked food so distracted her that she forgot. She was near the end of a second helping before she began to watch for the face behind the face; and to listen for the words hiding behind talk. It was Heed's fork play that finally pulled Junior's attention away from her own plate. Holding the fork between thumb and palm, driving leaves of Boston lettuce around oil and vinegar, piercing olives, lifting rings of onion on tines only to let them drop again and again, Heed had chattered on, eating nothing. Junior fixed on the hands more than on what occupied them: small, baby-smooth except for one scarred spot, each one curved gently away from its partner—like fins. Arthritis? she wondered. Is that why she can't write her own book? Or some other old-lady sickness? Memory loss, maybe. Even before the food arrived she had heard the change in Heed's speech, the slow move away from the classroom to the girls' locker; from a principal's office to a neighborhood bar.

Yawning under blankets in the bed to

which Heed had directed her, Junior fought sleep to organize, recapture her impressions. She knew she had eaten too much too quickly, as in her first days at Correctional before she learned how to make food last. And just as it had been there, she was already ready for more. Her appetite had not surprised her—it was permanent—but its ferocity had. Watching the gray-eyed Christine cleaning shrimp earlier, she had leashed it and had no trouble figuring out that a servant who cooked with twelve diamond rings on her fingers would enjoy—maybe even need—a little sucking up to. And although she had caught the other one's pose as well and recognized it from the start as a warden's righteous shield, Junior hoped that some up-front sass would crack it. Still, gobbling real food after days of clean garbage and public filch, she had let her antennae droop. As now, when sleep—alone, in silence, in total darkness at last—overwhelmed caution for pleasure. Simply not having a toilet in the room where you slept was a thrill. The bath she craved had to be postponed. When Heed said the weather was too nasty, the bus depot too far, and why not spend the night and collect your things tomorrow? Junior thought immediately of a solitary soak in a real tub with a perfumed bar of colored soap. But the water she heard running through pipes above reduced the tap flow in the second-floor bathtub to a sigh. Heed had beat her to it, so Junior spent a few minutes rummaging in the closet, where she found a helmet, one can of tomato paste, two rock-hard sacks of sugar, a jar of Jergens hand cream, a tin of sardines, a milk bottle full of keys, and two locked suitcases. She gave up trying to force the locks and undressed. After massaging her feet, she slid under the covers with two days' worth of dirt on hold.

Sleep came down so fast it was only in dreaming that she felt the peculiar new thing: protected. A faint trace of relief, as in the early days at Correctional when the nights were so terrifying; when upright snakes on tiny feet lay in wait, their thin green tongues begging her to come down from the tree. Once in a while there was someone beneath the branches standing apart from the snakes, and although she could not see who it was, his being there implied rescue. So she had endured the nightmares, even entered them, for a glimpse of the stranger's face. She never saw it, and eventually he disappeared along with the upright snakes. But here, now, deep in sleep, her search seemed to have ended. The face hanging over her new boss's bed must have started it. A handsome man with a G.I. Joe chin and a reassuring smile that pledged endless days of hot, tasty food; kind eyes that promised to hold a girl steady on his shoulder while she robbed apples from the highest branch.

2

FRIEND

Vida set up the ironing board. Why the hospital had cut out the laundry service for everybody except "critical staff"—doctors, nurses, lab technicians—she couldn't fathom. Now the janitors, food handlers, as well as the aides like herself, had to wash and press their own uniforms, reminding her of the cannery before Bill Cosey hired her away for the first work she ever had that required hosiery. She wore hose at the hospital, of course, but it was thick, white. Not the sheer, feminine ones preferred behind the receptionist's desk at Cosey's Hotel. Plus a really good dress, good enough for church. It was Bill Cosey who paid for two more, so she would have a change and the guests wouldn't confuse the wearing of one dress as a uniform. Vida thought he would deduct the cost from her pay, but he never did. His pleasure was in pleasing. "The best good time," he used to say. That was the resort's motto and what he promised every guest: "The best good time this side of the law." Vida's memories of working there merged with her childhood recollections of the hotel when famous people kept coming back. Even disturbances in the service or drowning accidents didn't dissuade them from extending their stay or returning the next year. All because of the beaming Bill Cosey and the wide hospitality his place was known for. His laugh, his embracing arm, his instinctive knowledge of his guests' needs smoothed over every crack or stumble, from an overheard argument among staff or a silly, overbearing wife—ignorant as a plate—to petty theft and a broken ceiling fan. Bill Cosey's charm and L's food won out. When the lamps ringing the dance floor were rocking in ocean air; when the band warmed up and the women appeared, dressed in moiré and chiffon and trailing jasmine scent in their wake; when the men with beautiful shoes and perfect creases in their linen trousers held chairs for the women so they could sit knee to knee at the little tables, then a missing saltcellar or harsh words exchanged much too near the public didn't matter. Partners swayed under the stars and didn't mind overlong intermissions because ocean breeze kept them happier and kinder than their cocktails. Later in the evening— when those who were not playing whist were telling big lies in the bar; when couples were sneaking off in the dark—the remaining dancers would do steps with outrageous names, names musicians made up to control, confuse, and excite their audiences all at the same time.

Vida believed she was a practical woman with as much sense as heart, more wary than dreamy. Yet she squeezed only sweetness from those nine years, beginning right after the birth of her only child, Dolly, in 1962. The decline under way even then was kept invisible until it was impossible to hide. Then Bill Cosey died and the Cosey girls fought over his coffin. Once again L restored order, just as she always had. Two words hissed into their faces stopped them cold. Christine closed the switchblade; Heed picked up her ridiculous hat and moved to the other side of the grave. Standing there, one to the right, one to the left, of Bill Cosey's casket, their faces, as differ-ent as honey from soot, looked identical. Hate does that. Burns off everything but itself, so whatever your grievance is, your face looks just like your enemy's. After that nobody could doubt the best good times were as dead as he was. If Heed had any notion of remaking the place into what it had been when Vida was a little Up Beach girl, she was quickly disabused of it when L quit that very day. She lifted a lily from the funeral spray and never set foot in the hotel again—not even to pack, collect her chef's hat or her white oxfords. In Sunday shoes with two-inch heels she walked from the cemetery all the way to Up Beach, claimed her mother's shack, and moved in. Heed did what she had to and what she could to keep it going, but a sixteen-year-old disc jockey working a tape player appealed only to locals. No one with real money would travel distance to hear it, would book a room to listen to the doo-wop tunes they had at home; would seek an open-air dance floor crowded with teenagers doing dances they never heard of and couldn't manage anyway. Especially if the meals, the service, the bed linen had to strain for an elegance unnoticed and unappreciated by the new crowd.

Vida slid the iron's nose around the buttons, frustrated once more by the slot in the metal that some male idiot thought would actually work. The same fool who believed a three-ounce iron was better than a heavy one. Lighter, yes, but it didn't iron anything that needed it, just things you could unwrinkle with your own warm hands: T-shirts, towels, cheap pillowcases. But not a good cotton uniform with twelve buttons, two cuffs, four pockets, and a collar that was not a lazy extension of the lapels. This was what she had come to? Vida knew she was lucky to have the hospital job. Slight as it was, her paycheck had helped fill her house with the sounds of gently helpful bells: time up in the microwave oven, the washing cycle, the spin dryer; watch out, there's smoke somewhere, the phone's off the hook. Lights glowed when coffee brewed, toast toasted, and the iron was hot. But the good fortune of her current job did not prevent her from preferring the long-ago one that paid less in every way but satisfaction. Cosey's Resort was more than a playground; it was a school and a haven where people debated death in the cities, murder in Mississippi, and what they planned to do about it other than grieve and stare at their children. Then the music started, convincing them they could manage it all and last.

She hung on, Heed did. Allow her that credit, but none other to a woman who gave torn towels and sheets to a flooded-out family instead of money. For years before Cosey actually died, while he aged and lost interest in everything but Nat Cole and Wild Turkey, Heed paraded around like an ignorant version of Scarlett O'Hara—refusing advice, firing the loyal, hiring the trifling, and fighting May, who was the one who really threatened her air supply. She couldn't fire her stepdaughter while Cosey was alive, even if he spent most days fishing and most nights harmonizing with tipsy friends. For it came to that: a commanding, beautiful man surrendering to feuding women, letting them ruin all he had built. How could they do that, Vida wondered. How could they let gangster types, dayworkers, cannery scum, and payday migrants in there, dragging police attention along with them like a tail? Vida had wanted to blame the increasingly raggedy clientele for May's kleptomania—Lord knows what those dayworkers took home—but May had been stealing even before Vida was hired and long before the quality of the guests changed. In fact, her second day at work, standing behind the desk, was marked by May's habit. A family of four from Ohio was checking in. Vida opened the registration book. The date, last name, and room number were neatly printed on the left, a space on the right for the guest's signature. Vida reached toward a marble pen stand but found no pen there or anywhere near. Flustered, she rummaged in a drawer. Heed arrived just as she was about to hand the father a pencil.

"What's that? You giving him a pencil?"

"The pen is missing, ma'am."

"It can't be. Look again."

"I have. It's not here."

"Did you look in your pocketbook?"

"Excuse me?"

"Your coat pocket, maybe?" Heed glanced at the guests and produced a resigned smile, as if they all understood the burdens of inadequate help. Vida was seventeen years old and a new mother. The position Mr. Cosey had given her was a high and, she hoped, permanent leap out of the fish trough where she used to work and her husband still did. Her mouth went dry and her fingers shook as Heed confronted her. Tears were marshaling to humiliate her further when rescue arrived, wearing a puffy white chef's hat. She held the fountain pen in her hand; stuck it in the holder, and, turning to Heed, said, "May. As you well know."

That's when Vida knew she had more to learn than registering guests and handling money. As in any workplace, there were old alliances here; mysterious battles, pathetic vic-

tories. Mr. Cosey was royal; L, the woman in
the chef's hat, priestly. All the rest—Heed,
Vida, May, waiters, cleaners—were court per-
sonnel fighting for the prince's smile.

She had surprised herself at the supper
table, bringing up that old gossip about
Cosey's death. Hating gossip bred of envy, she
wanted to believe what the doctor said: heart
attack. Or what L said: heartache. Or even
what May said: school busing. Certainly not
what his enemies said: syphilis rampant. Sandler said eighty-one years was enough; Bill
Cosey was simply tired. But Vida had seen the
water cloud before he drank it and his reach
not to his chest, where the heart exploded, but
to his stomach. Yet those who might have
wanted him dead—Christine, a husband or
two, and a few white businessmen—were
nowhere near. Just her, L, and one waiter. Lord,
what a mess. A dying body moves, thrashes
against that sleep. Then there was Heed
screaming like a maniac. May running off to
the Monarch Street house and locking herself
in a closet. Had it not been for L, the county's
role model would never have gotten the digni-
fied funeral he deserved. Even when Christine
and Heed almost trashed it at the end, L
stepped between those rigid vipers, forcing
them to bite back their tongues. Which, by all

reports, they were still doing, while waiting for the other one to die. So the girl Sandler directed to their house must be related to Heed. She was the only one with living family. With five brothers and three sisters there could be fifty nieces. Or maybe she wasn't a relative at all. Vida decided to ask Romen to find out—discreetly, if he could; otherwise directly, although there was little hope of a reliable answer from him. The boy was so inattentive these days, so moody. A furlough for one of his parents right about now would be welcome, before he got into trouble neither she nor Sandler could handle. His hands hadn't gotten that way from yard work. He beat somebody. Bad.

Beneath the house under the light of a single bulb, Sandler chuckled. Vida was on her game. He *had* been struck by the girl's legs. In freezing wind, not a goose bump in view—just tight, smooth skin with the promise of strong muscle underneath. Dancer's legs: long, unhappy at rest, eager to lift, to spread, to wrap themselves around you. He should be ashamed, he thought, as the chuckle grew into smothered laughter: an over-fifty grandfather faithful and devoted to his wife giggling into a boiler dial in the cellar, happy to be arousable by the unexpected sight of young thighs. He knew his gruffness with her had been a reaction to the feelings she stirred and believed she knew it too.

Sandler peered at the dial, wondering if an 80-degree setting would be likely to produce 70 degrees in his bedroom, since the current 70-degree setting was equaling 60 degrees there. He sighed over the problem: a furnace seldom needed in that climate seemed as confused about its workings as he was. And sighed again as he recalled the underdressed girl who must be a northerner indifferent to 30 degrees. He could not imagine what she wanted with either one of those Cosey women. He would ask Romen to check it out. Or maybe not. Asking his grandson to spy would introduce the wrong element into a relationship already lopsided with distrust. He wanted Romen upright—not sneaking around women on some frivolous errand. It would undermine his moral authority. Still, if the boy happened to report something, he would be as pleased to hear it as anybody. The Coseys had always been a heated topic. In these parts—Ocean-side, Sooker Bay, Up Beach, Silk—their goings-on had splattered conversation for fifty years. Naturally so, since the resort affected them all. Provided them with work other than fish and pack crab; attracted outsiders who offered years of titillation and agitated talk. Otherwise they never saw anybody but themselves. The withdrawal of that class of tourist was hard on everyone, like a receding wave that left shells and kelp script, scattered and unreadable, behind.

There were cold spots in the Oceanside house, places the heat seemed never to enter. Hot spots too. And all of his tinkering with thermostats and base heating and filters was just that—tinkering. Like his neighbors', his house was built as a gesture: two-inch nails instead of four, lightweight roofing guaranteed for ten years instead of thirty, single-thickness panes rattling in their molding. Each year Sandler became fonder of the neighborhood he and Vida had moved away from. She had been right, certainly, to leave Up Beach when they did, before the drought that ended in flood, and she never gave it another thought. As he did almost every day, as now, on a very cold night, longing for the crackle of fire in a stingy potbelly stove, the smell of clean driftwood burning. He couldn't forget the picture the moon turned those Up Beach cabins into. Here, in this government-improved and -approved housing with too much man-made light, the moon did nothing kind. The planners believed that dark people would do fewer dark things if there were twice as many streetlamps as anywhere else. Only in fine neighborhoods and the country were people entrusted to shadow. So even when the moon was full and blazing, for Sandler it was like a bounty hunter's far-off torch, not the blanket of beaten gold it once spread over him and the ramshackle house of his childhood, exposing the trick of the world, which is to make us think it is ours. He wanted his own moon again releasing a wide gold finger to travel the waves and point directly at him. No matter where he stood on the beach, it knew exactly; as unwavering and personal as a mother's touch, the gold finger found him, knew him. And although he understood that it came from a cold stone incapable even of indifference, he also knew it was pointing to him alone and nobody else. Like the windblown girl who had singled him out, breaking out of evening wind to stand between garage light and sunset, backlit, spotlighted, and looking only at him.

Bill Cosey would have done more. Invited her in to warm herself, offered to drive her where she wanted to go, instead of barking at her, doubting her accuracy. Cosey would have succeeded, too; he almost always did. Vida, like

so many others, had looked on him with ador-
ing eyes, spoke of him with forgiving smiles.
Proud of his finesse, his money, the example he
set that goaded them into thinking that with
patience and savvy, they could do it too. But
Sandler had fished with him, and while he did
not claim to know his heart, mind, or wallet,
he knew his habits.

They were lee, bobbing in a cove, not out to
deep sea as he had expected.

Sandler had been surprised by the invitation, since Cosey usually shared his boat only
with special guests, or, most often, the sheriff,
Buddy Silk—one member of a family that had
named a whole town after itself and gave
epic-movie names to its streets. Cosey had
approached him in the road where Sandler was
parked waiting for Vida. He aligned his pale
blue Impala with Sandler's pickup and said,
"You busy tomorrow, Sandler?"

"No, sir."

"Not working?"

"No, sir. Cannery's closed on Sunday."

"Oh, right."

"You need me for something?"

Cosey pursed his lips as though second-
guessing his invitation, then turned his face
away.

Sandler contemplated his profile, which

looked like the one on a nickel minus the
hairdo and feathers. Still handsome, Cosey was
seventy-four years old then; Sandler twenty-
two. Cosey had been married over twenty
years; Sandler less than three. Cosey had
money; Sandler earned one dollar and seventy
cents an hour. He wondered if any two men
had less to talk about.

Having come to a decision, Cosey faced
Sandler.

"I aim to fish a little. First light. Thought
you might like to join me."

Working fish all day, Sandler did not con-
nect catching them with sport. He'd rather
shoot than fish, but there was no way to
decline. Vida wouldn't like it, besides he had
heard that Cosey's boat was smart.

"You don't need to bring anything. I have it
all."

You can say that again, thought Sandler.

They met at the pier at 4 a.m. and pushed
off immediately, in silence. No weather chat or
wagers about the haul. Cosey seemed less
hearty than the evening before. Sandler put the
change down to the seriousness of handling
the little cruiser, tacking into the ocean, then
landward to a cove Sandler knew nothing
about. Or else it was the oddity of their being
alone together. Cosey didn't mix with local

people publicly, which is to say he employed them, joked with them, even rescued them from difficult situations, but other than at church picnics, none was truly welcome at the hotel's tables or on its dance floor. Back in the forties, price kept most neighborhood people away, but even when a family collected enough money to celebrate a wedding there, they were refused. Pleasantly. Regretfully. Definitely. The hotel was booked. There was some spotty rancor over the undisguised rejection, but in those days most didn't mind, thought it reasonable. They had neither the clothes nor the funds, and did not wish to be embarrassed by those who did. When Sandler was a boy, it was enough to watch the visitors, admire their cars and the quality of their luggage; to listen to the distant music and dance to it in the dark, the deep dark, between their own houses, in shadow underneath their own windowsills. It was enough to know Bill Cosey's Hotel and Resort was there. Otherwise, how to explain the comfort available nowhere else in the county, or the state, for that matter. Cannery workers and fishing families prized it. So did housemaids traveling to Silk, laundresses, fruit pickers, as well as teachers in broken-down schools; even visiting ministers, who did not hold with liquor-fueled gatherings or dance music—all felt a tick of entitlement, of longing turned to belonging in the vicinity of the fabulous, successful resort controlled by one of their own. A fairy tale that lived on even after the hotel was dependent for its life on the people it once excluded.

"Bonito come back in here," said Cosey. "Way station for them, I guess." He brightened and pulled out a thermos of coffee that, Sandler discovered, was so laced the coffee was more color than flavor. It did the trick. They were soon deep in the merits of Cassius Clay, which quelled an argument about Medgar Evers.

The catch was poor, the banter jovial, until sunrise, when the alcohol leveled and the talk turned gloomy. Cosey, looking at some lively worms in the belly of a catfish, said, "If you kill the predators, the weak will eat you alive."

"Everything has its place, Mr. Cosey," Sandler replied.

"True. Everything. Except women. They're all over the damn place."

Sandler laughed.

"In the bed," continued Cosey, "the kitchen, the yard, at your table, under your feet, on your back."

"That can't be all bad," offered Sandler.

"No. No. It's great. Great."

"Then why ain't you smiling?"

Bill Cosey turned to look at Sandler. His eyes, though bright from drink, radiated pain like cracked glass. "What do they say about me?" he asked, sipping from the thermos.

"They?"

"You all. You know. Behind my back."

"You a highly respected man, Mr. Cosey."

Cosey sighed as though the answer disappointed him. "Damned if I do, damned if I don't," he said. Then, in the sudden shift of subject that children and heavy drinkers enjoy, "My son, Billy, was about your age. When he died, I mean."

"Is that right?"

"We had some good times. Good times. More like pals than father and son. When I lost him . . . it was like somebody from the grave reached up and grabbed him for spite."

"Somebody?"

"I mean something."

"How'd he die?"

"Damnedest thing. Walking pneumonia they call it. No symptoms. A cough or two and the lights go out." He scowled into the water as though the mystery was floating down there. "I lost it for a while. Took a long time to get over it."

"But you did. Get over it."

"I did," he answered, smiling. "A pretty woman came along and the clouds just drifted off."

"See there. And you complaining."

"You're right. Still, I was so caught up with him, I never took the trouble to know him. I used to wonder why he picked a woman like May to marry. Maybe he was somebody else and I made him my . . . shadow. And now I'm thinking *I* don't understand anybody. So why should anybody understand me?"

"Hard to know people. All you can go by is what they do," Sandler said, wondering, Is he trying to say he's lonesome, misunderstood? Worrying about a son dead for twenty-some years? This man, with more friends than honey had bees, worrying about his reputation? With women fighting so hard for his attention you'd think he was a preacher. And he moaning about the burden of it? Sandler decided the whiskey had pushed Cosey to the crying phase. It had to be that, otherwise he was in the company of a fool. He could swallow hot rocks easier than he could the complaints of a rich man. Vaguely insulted, Sandler turned his attention to the bait box. If he waited long enough, Cosey would skip to another topic.

Which he did, after singing a few refrains of a Platters song.

"Do you know that every law in this country is made to keep us back?"

Sandler looked up, thinking, Where did that come from? He laughed. "That can't be true."

"Oh, but it is."

"What about . . ." but Sandler couldn't remember any laws about anything except murder, and that wouldn't help his case. Everybody knew who went to prison and who didn't. A black killer was a killer; a white killer was unhappy. He felt sure that most law was about money, not color, and said so.

Cosey answered with a slow wink. "Think about that," he said. "A Negro can have A-one credit, solid collateral, and not a hope in hell of a bank loan. Think about that."

Sandler didn't want to. His marriage was fresh, his daughter new. Vida was all he knew of A-one; Dolly was all he needed for hope.

That was their first of many fishing trips, confidences. Eventually Cosey persuaded Sandler to stop cleaning crab at the cannery. With tips, waiting tables at the hotel would put more in his pocket. Sandler tried it for a few months, but in 1966, with riots in any big city you could name, a cannery boss offered him a supervisory job, hoping the gesture would forestall any restlessness that might infect the all-black labor force. It worked out. Cosey felt easier in a friendship between himself and a foreman than with one of his own waiters. But the more Sandler learned about the man, the less he knew. At times sympathy conquered disappointment; other times dislike overcame affection. Like the time Cosey told him a story, something about how when he was little his father made him play in a neighbor's yard to see who came out the back door. Every dawn he was sent to watch. A man did slip out one day and Cosey reported it to his father. That afternoon he saw the man dragged through the street behind a four-horse wagon.

"You helped catch a thief, a killer?" Sandler asked in admiration.

"Yep."

"Good for you."

"Bunch of kids ran after the wagon, crying. One was a little girl. Raggedy as Lazarus. She tripped in some horse shit and fell. People laughed."

"What'd you do?"

"Nothing. Nothing at all."

"You were a kid."

"Yeah."

During the telling, Sandler's quick sympathy changed to embarrassment when he wondered if Cosey laughed too. Other times he felt active dislike for the man, as when he refused to sell land to local people. Folks were divided on whether to blame him or his wife for selling it to a developer cashing in on HUD money. By way of fish fries, bake sales, rummage sales, and tithing, they had collected enough for a deposit. They planned some kind of cooperative: small businesses, Head Start, cultural centers for arts, crafts, classes in Black History and Self-defense. At first Cosey was willing, but he stalled the deal so long the decision was left to his widow. She sold it off before his tombstone was set. When Sandler and others moved to Oceanside, he was still of two minds about Cosey. Knowing him, watching him, was not so much about changing his mind; it was more like an education. At first he thought Cosey was a dollar man. At least people said he was, and he certainly spent his money as though they were right. Yet a year or so into those fishing trips, Sandler began to see Cosey's wealth not as a hammer wielded by a tough-minded man, but more like the toy of a sentimental one. Rich people could act like sharks, but what drove them was a kid's sweet tooth. Childish yearnings that could thrive only in a meadow of girlish dreams: adoration, obedience, and full-time fun. Vida believed a powerful, generous friend gazed out from the portrait hanging behind the reception desk. That was because she didn't know who he was looking at.

Sandler climbed the stairs from the basement. The early retirement he'd been forced to take had seemed like a good idea at the time. Walking malls at midnight rested the mind without slowing it. Now he wondered if there was brain damage he hadn't counted on, since he was becoming more and more fixed on the past rather than the moment he stood in. When he entered the kitchen, Vida was folding clothes and singing along to some bluesy country music on the radio. Thinking, maybe, of those cracked-glass eyes rather than the ones in the painting, he grabbed her shoulders, turned her around, and held on tight while they danced.

Maybe his girlish tears were worse than the reason he shed them. Maybe they were a weakness the others recognized and pinpointed even before he punked out. Even before the melt had flooded his chest when he saw her hands, curving down from the snow white shoelaces that bound them. They might have

been mittens pinned crookedly on a clothes-
line, hung there by some slut who didn't care
what the neighbors said. And the plum polish
on nails bitten to the quick gave the mitten-
tiny hands a womanly look and made Romen
think she herself was the slut—the one with
no regard for what people might think.

He was next in line. And ready, too, in spite
of the little hands and in spite of the mewing
in her throat. He stood near the headboard
charged by Theo's brays and his head bobbing
above the girl's face, which was turned to the
wall and hidden beneath hair undone by
writhing. His belt unbuckled, anticipation
ripe, he was about to become the Romen he'd
always known he was: chiseled, dangerous,
loose. Last of a group of seven. Three had left as
soon as they were finished—slapping fives on
their way out of the bedroom and back to
where the party raged. Freddie and Jamal sat
on the floor, spent but watching as Theo, who
had been first, took seconds. Slower this time,
his whinny the only sound because the girl
wasn't mewing anymore. By the time he with-
drew, the room smelled of vegetables and rot-
ten grapes and wet clay. Only the silence was
fresh.

Romen stepped forward to take Theo's
place, then watched in wonder as his hands

moved to the headboard. The knot binding her right wrist came undone as soon as he touched it and her hand fell over the bedside. She did not use it at all—not to hit or scratch or push back her hair. Romen untied the other hand still hanging from the Pro Ked laces. Then he wrapped her in the spread she was lying on and hoisted her into a sitting position. He picked up her shoes, high-heeled, an X of pink leather across the front—good for nothing but dancing and showing off. He could hear the whooping laughter—that came first—then the jokes and finally the anger, but he got her out of there through the dancing crowd and onto the porch. Trembling, she held on tight to the shoes he handed her. If either had been drunk earlier, they weren't anymore. A cold wind took their breath away.

He thought her name was Faye or Faith and was about to say something when suddenly he couldn't stand the sight of her. If she thanked him, he would strangle her. Fortunately, she didn't say a word. Eyes frozen wide, she put on her shoes and straightened her skirt. Both of their coats, his new leather jacket and whatever she had worn, were inside the house.

The door opened; two girls ran out, one carrying a coat, the other holding up a purse.

"Pretty-Fay! What happened?"

Romen turned to go.

"What happened to you, girl? Hey, you! You do something to her?"

Romen kept walking.

"Come back here! He bother you? Well, who? Who? Look at your hair! Here, put your coat on. Pretty-Fay! Say something, girl!"

He heard their shrieks, their concern, as cymbal clashes, stressing, but not competing with, the trumpet blast of what Theo had called him: the worst name there was; the one word whose reverberation, once airborne, only a fired gun could end. Otherwise there was no end—ever.

For the past three days he had been a joke. His easily won friendship—four months old now—lost. Holding the stare of any one of the six others, except for Freddie, was a dare, an invitation, and even when he didn't stare back or meet their eyes at all, the trumpet spoke his name. They gathered without him at the link fence; left the booth at Patty's Burgers when he sat down. Even the flirtiest girls sensed his undesirability, as though all at once his clothes were jive: T-shirt too white, pants too pressed; sneakers laced all wrong.

On the first day following the party, nobody refused him court time but he never got a pass and when he intercepted he had to try for a dunk wherever his position because there was no one to receive the ball. They dropped their hands and looked at him. If he made a rebound they fouled it away from him and the trumpet spat before he could see who blew it. Finally they just tripped him and walked off the court. Romen sat there, panting, eager to fight but knowing that if he answered the fouls, the tripping, the trumpet spit, it would be the same as defending the girl again. Somebody he didn't know and didn't want to. If he fought back, he would be fighting not for himself, but for her, Pretty-Fay; proving the connection between them—the wrong connection. As though he *and* her had been tied to a bed; his legs *and* hers forced open.

Lucas Breen, one of the white boys whose hoop skill was envied, dribbled and shot all alone at the far end of the court. Romen got up and started to join him, but realized in time that there was another word in the trumpet's repertoire. He passed Lucas with a glance, muttering, "Hey."

The second day was miserable, lonelier. Freddie brought him the jacket he'd left and said, "Hey, man. Don't get shook," but didn't hang around to say more. After he saw Pretty-Fay's friends, the two who had come running out with her coat and purse, waving at him through the window of the school bus, he began to ride the commuter bus. Readily he chose the inconvenience of walking two miles to and from the stop to avoid the possibility of seeing Pretty-Fay herself. He never did. Nor did anyone else.

The third day they beat him up. All six, including Freddie. Smart, too. They hit him everywhere except his face, just in case he was a snitch as well, happy to explain a broken mouth or swollen eye; girl enough to point a weak finger at them if questioned. All six. Romen fought well; raised a lump or two, kneed deep into a groin, tore a shirt till they got his hands behind his back and tried to break his ribs and empty his stomach at the same time. That last was starting to happen when a car drove up and honked. Everybody scattered, including Romen, who stumbled away holding his stomach, more fearful of being rescued than of passing out with vomit on his jeans. He threw up behind a mimosa tree in the woods back of Patty's. Contemplating his grandmother's cooking in the grass, he began to wonder if he could ever live his body down. He did not question Theo's sneering or Freddie's disgust; he shared both, and couldn't understand what had made him melt at that moment—his heart bursting like a pump for a wounded creature who a few seconds earlier had been a feast he was eager to gnaw. If he'd found her in the street, his reaction would have been the same, but in the company of and part of the pack who put her there—shit! What was that thing that had moved him to untie her, cover her, Jesus! Cover her! Cover her up! Get her on her feet and out of there? The little mitten hands? The naked male behinds convulsing one after another after another after another? The vegetable odor mixed with a solid booming bass on the other side of the door? As he put his arm around her and led her away, he was still erect, folding only as they stepped together out into the cold. What made him do it? Or rather, who?

But he knew who it was. It was the real Romen who had sabotaged the newly chiseled, dangerous one. The fake Romen, preening over a stranger's bed, was tricked by the real Romen, who was still in charge here in his own bed, forcing him to hide under a pillow and shed girl tears. The trumpet stuttering in his head.

3

STRANGER

The Settlement is a planet away from One Monarch Street. A little huddle, a bit of sprawl, it has claimed the slope of a mountain and the valley below since World War I. No one uses its name—not the post office or the Census Bureau. The State Troopers know it well, however, and a few people who used to work in the old Relief Office have heard of it, but the new employees of the County Welfare Office have not. From time to time, teachers in District Ten have had students from there, but they don't use the word "Settlement." "Rurals" is what these strange unteachable children are labeled. Although they infuriated ordinary students from decent farming families, Guidance Counselors had to choose some socially benign term to identify these children without antagonizing their parents, who might get wind of it. The term proved satisfactory, although no Settlement parent ever appeared to request, permit, observe, consult, or complain. Notes or forms placed in their children's unsoaped hands were never returned or responded to. Rurals sat in class for a few months, sharing textbooks, borrowing paper and pencils, but purposefully silent as though they were there to test, not acquire, education; to witness, not supply, information. They were quiet in the classroom and kept to themselves, partly out of choice and partly because they were carefully avoided by their peers. Rurals were known as sudden fighters—relentless and vicious. It was common knowledge that sometime in the late fifties a principal managed to locate, then visit, the home of a Rural named Otis Rick. Otis had loosened a child's eye on the playground and had not understood or obeyed the expelled notice stuck in his shirt pocket. He had come back every day, his victim's dried blood still on his sleeves. Not much is known of this official visit to demand Otis's permanent absence—except one vivid detail. When the principal left the Rick property, he had to cover the whole length of the valley on foot because he had been given no time or chance to get back in his car. The DeSoto was towed back to town by State Troopers because nothing could make its owner go back to retrieve it.

Very old people who were young during the Great Depression, and who still call that part of the county "the Settlement," could describe the history of its inhabitants, if anyone asked. But as their opinions are seldom sought, Settlement people have it the way they want it: unevolved and reviled, they are also tolerated, left alone, and feared. Quite the way it was in 1912 when the jute mill was abandoned and those who could leave left and those who could not (the black ones because they had no hope, or the white ones who had no prospects) lolled on, marrying one another, sort of, and figuring out how to stay alive from day to day. They built their own houses from other people's scraps, or they added on to the workers' cabins left by the jute company: a shed here, a room there, to the cluster of little two-room-and-a-stove huts that wavered on the slope or sat in the valley. They used stream and rain water, drank cow's milk or home brew; ate game, eggs, domestic plants, and if they hired out in a field or a kitchen, they spent the earnings on sugar, salt, cooking oil, soda pop, cornflakes, flour, dried beans, and rice. If there were no earnings, they stole.

Unlike the tranquillity of its name, the Settlement heaved with loyalty and license, and the only crime was departure. One such treason was undertaken by a girl with merged toes called Junior. Her mother, Vivian, had meant to name her right away. Three days had passed after the hard delivery before she could stay awake long enough to make a decision—during which time the baby girl's father called the newborn "Junior," either after himself—Ethan Payne Jr.—or after his longing, for although Vivian already had four boy children, none of them was Ethan's. Vivian finally did choose a name for the baby and may even have used it once or twice after Ethan moved back to his father's house. But "Junior" stuck. Nothing more was required until the child entered District Ten and a last name was demanded of her. "Junior Vivian," she murmured, and when the teacher smiled into her hand, the girl scratched her elbow, having just realized she could have said "June."

Settlement girls were discouraged from schooling, but each of Junior's uncles, male cousins, and half brothers had spent some time at District Ten. Unlike any one of them, she was seldom truant. At home, with no one or anyone in charge, she felt like one of the Settlement dogs. Fifty strong, they swung between short chains and unfettered roaming. Between fights and meals they slept lashed to trees or curled near a door. Left to their own devices, hounds mated with shepherds, collies with Labradors. By 1975, when Junior was born, they were an odd, original, astonishingly handsome breed instantly recognizable to folks who knew as Settlement dogs—adept at keeping outsiders out, but at their brilliant best when hunting.

During years of longing for her father, Junior begged relentlessly to visit him.

"Will you hush up?" was all Vivian said, until one day she answered, "Army. That's what I heard."

"When's he coming back?"

"Oh, he weren't nothing, baby. Nothing at all. Go play now."

She did, but she kept on looking out for the tall, handsome man who named her after himself to show how he felt about her. She just had to wait.

Bored at last with the dogs and her mother, faster and slyer than her brothers, afraid of her uncles and unamused by their wives, Junior welcomed District Ten, first to get away from the Settlement, then for itself. She was the first Rural to speak up and make a stab at homework. The girls in her class avoided her and the few who tried to sprinkle the seeds of friendship were quickly forced to choose between the untidy Rural with one dress and the crafty vengeance little girls know how to exact. Junior lost every time, but behaved as though the rejection was her victory, smiling when she saw the one-recess friend retreat to her original fold. It was a boy who succeeded at befriending her. The teachers thought it was because he fed her Yodels and Sno Balls from his lunch bag, since Junior's lunch might be a single apple or a mayonnaise sandwich stuffed in the pocket of the woman's sweater she wore. The pupils, however, believed he was playing dirty with her down in a ditch somewhere after school—and they told him so. But he was a proud boy, son of the bottling-plant manager, who could hire and fire their parents—and he told them so.

His name was Peter Paul Fortas, and having lived through eleven years of being called Pee Pee, he had grown insolent and unyielding to popular opinion. Peter Paul and Junior were not interested in each other's bodies. Junior wanted to know about vats of Coke syrup and capping machines. Peter Paul wanted to know if it was true about brown bears on the mountain and whether it was the calves or the smell of milk that attracted snakes. They traded information like racetrack tipsters, skipping biography to get to the meat of the game. Once, however, he asked her if she was Colored. Junior said she didn't know but would find out for him. He said it didn't matter, because he couldn't invite Gentiles to his house anyway. He didn't want her feelings hurt. She nodded, pleased with the serious, pretty word he had called her.

He pilfered for her: a ballpoint pen, a pair of socks, a yellow barrette for her finger-combed hair. When, for Christmas, she gave him a baby cottonmouth curled in a bottle and he gave her a jumbo box of crayons, it was hard to tell which one was happier.

But the cottonmouth was a snake, after all, and it did them in.

Some of Junior's uncles, idle teenagers whose brains had been insulted by the bleakness of their lives, alternated between brutality and coma. They did not believe the jarred snake had been for a class assignment, as Junior told them when asked, "What's 'et you hauling off, gal?" Or if they did believe her, the act was deeply offensive to them. Something belonging to the Settlement was being transferred to

the site of a failure so dismal it had not registered on them as failure at all—but as the
triumph of natural light over institutional
darkness. Or perhaps it was too late for pos-
sum, or one of them had not shared his beer.
Whatever the reason, the uncles were wide
awake the morning after Christmas and fun-
seeking.

Junior was asleep, her head on a stained
"Jesus Saves" pillow, wrapped in a blanket
serving also as a mattress. The pillow, a Christmas gift from an uncle's wife who got it from
the trash box of her then-employer, encouraged dreams. The crayons, held to her chest,
decorated them. So colorful was her sleep, an
uncle had to tap her behind with his boot
more than once to wake her. They questioned
her about the snake again. The crayon-colored
dreams drained slowly as Junior tried to figure
out what they wanted, there being no point in
wondering the why of anything with them.
They didn't know themselves why they set fire
to a car seat rather than remove it. Or why a
snake was important to them. They wanted the
cottonmouth returned to its rightful home.

Among the threats if she didn't go get it
were "to break your pretty little butt" and
"hand you over to Vosh." This latter she had
heard many times before, and the possibility

that it could happen, that she could be handed over to the old man in the valley who liked to walk around with his private parts in his hand singing hymns of praise, jolted her up from the floor, out of reaching hands and through the door. The uncles chased her, but she was swift. Chained dogs growled; loose ones joined in. On her way down the path, she saw Vivian returning from the privy.

"Ma!" she called.

"Leave her 'lone, you goddamn polecats!" screamed Vivian. She took a few running steps before fatigue ended in futile rock-throwing at the backs of her younger brothers. "Leave her 'lone! Come back here, you skunks! You better mind me!"

Urgent, heartfelt if not optimistic, the words were a comfort to the running girl. Barefoot, clutching a jumbo box of crayons, Junior dodged, hid from, and managed to lose the howling uncles. She found herself in the kind of wood lumbermen salivate over. Pecans the size of which had not been seen since the twenties. Maples boasting six and seven trunk-size arms. Locusts, butternut, white cedar, ash. Healthy trees mixed with sick ones. Huge black cauliflowers of disease grew on some. Others looked healthy until a wind, light and playful, ruffled their crown. Then they cracked and fell like coronary victims, copper and gold meal pouring from the break.

Darting, then pausing, Junior arrived at a sunlit stand of bamboo strangling in Virginia creeper. The howling had stopped. She waited, then climbed a Northern Spy to scan the mountainside and what she could see of the valley. No uncles in sight. Just the parting of trees where the creek ran. And beyond it the road.

The sun was high when she got to its edge. Of no importance to her were flesh cuts or twigs embedded in her hair, but she mourned the seven crayons broken in flight before she got to use even one. Vivian could not protect her from Vosh or the uncles, so she decided to find Peter Paul's house, wait for him somewhere nearby, and—what? Well, he would help her somehow. But she would never, ever, ask him to return the baby cottonmouth.

She stepped out onto the road and had not gone fifty feet when a truckful of uncles clattered behind her. She jumped left, of course, instead of right, but they had anticipated that. When the front fender knocked her sideways, the rear tire crushed her toes.

A bumpy ride in the bed of the truck, a place on Vivian's cot, whiskey in her mouth, camphor in her nose—nothing woke her until the pain ratcheted down to unbearable. Junior opened her eyes to fever and a hurt so stunning she could not fill her lungs. Breath came and went in thimblefuls. Day after day she lay there, first unable, then refusing, to cry or speak to Vivian, who was telling her how thankful she should be that the uncles had found her sprawled on the roadside, her baby girl Junior struck down by a car driven, no doubt, by a town bastard too biggedy to stop after running over a little girl and check to see if she was dead or leastwise give her a lift.

In silence Junior watched her toes swell, redden, turn blue, then black, then marble, then merge. The crayons were gone and the hand that once held them now clutched a knife ready for Vosh or an uncle or anyone stopping her from committing the Settlement version of crime: leaving, getting out. Clean away from people who chased her down, ran over her foot, lied about it, called her lucky, and who preferred the company of a snake to a girl. In one year she was gone. Two more and she was fed, bathed, clothed, educable, and thriving. Behind bars.

Junior was eleven when she ran away and wandered for weeks without attention being paid. Then suddenly noticed when she stole a G.I. Joe doll from an "Everything for a Dollar" store, taken into custody when she wouldn't give it back, transferred to a shelter when she bit the woman who yanked it from her, remanded to Correctional when she refused to provide any information other than her first name. "Junior Smith," they wrote, and "Junior Smith" she remained until the state let her go and she reclaimed her true name with an *e* added for style.

Some of the education at Correctional was academic; most of it was not. Both kinds honed the cunning needed to secure a place in a big, fancy house on Monarch Street where there was no uniformed woman pacing in the half-light of a corridor or opening doors any old time to check; or where the sleep thrum of bodies close by siphoned the air. This was the right place and there he was, letting her know in every way it had been waiting for her all along. As soon as she saw the stranger's portrait she knew she was home. She had dreamed him the first night, had ridden his shoulders through an orchard of green Granny apples heavy and thick on the boughs.

The next morning at breakfast—grapefruit, scrambled eggs, grits, toast, bacon—Christine was less hostile but still guarded. Junior tried to amuse her by poking fun at Heed. The lay of the land, so to speak, was not entirely clear, and she had no direction. It was when she'd finished eating and was back in Heed's bedroom that she knew for sure. The gift was unmistakable.

Awkward in Heed's red suit, Junior had stood at the window and looked again at the boy below while Heed rummaged in a footlocker. Earlier she had seen Christine shoot down the driveway, leaving the boy holding a pail and shivering in the yard. Now she watched him wipe his nose with the back of his wrist, then brush the residue on his jeans. Junior smiled. And was smiling still when Heed called out to her.

"Here it is! I found it." She held a photograph in a silver frame. "I keep valuables locked up in one place or another and sometimes I forget where."

Junior left the window, knelt next to the footlocker, and gazed at the photograph. A wedding. Five people. And him, the groom, looking to his right at a woman who, holding a single rose, focused a frozen smile at the camera.

"She looks like the woman downstairs, Christine," said Junior, pointing.

"Well, she's not," said Heed.

The woman with the rose held his arm, and although he was looking at her, his other arm was around the bare shoulder of his tiny bride. Heed was swamped by the oversize wedding gown falling from her shoulders and the orange blossoms in her hand were drooping. To Heed's left was a slick-looking handsome man smiling to *his* left at a woman whose clenched hands emphasized more than the absence of a bouquet.

"I don't look so different, do I?" asked Heed.

"Why is your husband looking at her and not you?"

"Trying to cheer her up, I suppose. He was like that."

"That your bridesmaid?" asked Junior, pointing to the clench-fisted woman. "She doesn't look too happy either."

"She wasn't. Can't say it was a happy wedding. Bill Cosey was very marriage-ing, you know. A lot of women wanted to be in my slippers."

Junior examined the picture again. "Who's that other guy?"

"Our best man. A very famous musician in his day. You too young to know about him."

"These the people you're writing about?"

"Yes. Well, some. Mostly about Papa—my husband—his people, his father. You wouldn't believe how proud they were, how classy. Even back in slavery days . . ."

There was more than one reason Junior stopped listening. One was that she guessed Heed didn't want to write a book; she wanted to talk, although why she had to pay somebody to talk to, Junior hadn't figured out yet. The other was the boy shivering outside. She could hear the faint scrapes of his shovel moving slush, tapping ice.

"Does he live around here?"

"Who?"

"Kid outside."

"Oh, that's Sandler's boy. He runs errands, keeps the yard up. Nice boy."

"What's his name?"

"Romen. His grandfather was a friend to my husband. They fished together. Papa had two boats, you know. One named for his first wife, and one named for me . . ."

Sixteen, maybe older. Nice neck.

". . . he took important people deep-sea fishing. The sheriff, Chief Silk, they called him. He was Papa's best friend. And big-name singers, bandleaders. But he took Sandler, too, even though he was just a local man working in the cannery like most everybody then. But Papa could mix with all kinds . . ."

He won't like this old-lady suit I got on.

"People just adored him and he was good to everybody. Of course, his will left me the most, though to hear some people, a wife shouldn't be provided for ..."

Like the boys at Campus A shooting baskets, and us looking at them through the wire fence, daring them. Them looking back at us, promising us.

"I was lucky, I know that. My mother was against it at first. Papa's age and all. But Daddy knew a true romance when he saw it. And look how it turned out. Almost thirty years of perfect bliss ..."

The Guards were jealous. Roughing them up because we kept on looking, greedy, like fans, watching those damp sweats rise.

"Neither one of us even looked at anybody else. But it sure wasn't easy-greasy running the hotel. Everything was on me. With nobody to count on. Nobody ..."

Sixteen at least, maybe more. Shoots baskets, too. I can tell.

"Are you listening to me? I'm giving you important information. You should be writing all this down."

"I'll remember."

Half an hour later, Junior had changed back into leather. When Romen saw her walking up the driveway, he thought what his grandfather must have thought, and grinned in spite of himself.

Junior liked that. Then, suddenly, like the boys at Campus A, he slouched—indifferent, ready to be turned down, ready to pounce. Junior didn't give him time to decide on the matter.

"Don't tell me you're fucking these old women too."

Too.

Romen's embarrassment fought with a flush of pride. She assumed he was capable of it. Of having scored so many times he could choose any woman—and in pairs, Theo, in pairs.

"They tell you that?"

"No. But I bet they think about it."

"You related to them?"

"No way. I work here now."

"Doing what?"

"This and that."

"What kinda this? What kinda that?"

Junior circled her gift. She looked at the shovel in his hands. Then his crotch, then his face. "They got rooms they never go in. With sofas and everything."

"Yeah?"

LOVE

• • •

*Young people, Lord. Do they still call it infatuation?
That magic ax that chops away the world in one
blow, leaving only the couple standing there trembling? Whatever they call it, it leaps over anything,
takes the biggest chair, the largest slice, rules the
ground wherever it walks, from a mansion to a
swamp, and its selfishness is its beauty. Before I was
reduced to singsong, I saw all kinds of mating. Most
are two-night stands trying to last a season. Some,
the riptide ones, claim exclusive right to the real
name, even though everybody drowns in its wake.
People with no imagination feed it with sex—the
clown of love. They don't know the real kinds, the
better kinds, where losses are cut and everybody
benefits. It takes a certain intelligence to love like
that—softly, without props. But the world is such a
showpiece, maybe that's why folks try to outdo it,
put everything they feel onstage just to prove they
can think up things too: handsome scary things like
fights to the death, adultery, setting sheets afire. They
fail, of course. The world outdoes them every time.
While they are busy showing off, digging other people's graves, hanging themselves on a cross, running
wild in the streets, cherries are quietly turning from
green to red, oysters are suffering pearls, and children
are catching rain in their mouths expecting the drops
to be cold but they're not; they are warm and smell*

like pineapple before they get heavier and heavier, so heavy and fast they can't be caught one at a time. Poor swimmers head for shore while strong ones wait for lightning's silver veins. Bottle-green clouds sweep in, pushing the rain inland where palm trees pretend to be shocked by the wind. Women scatter shielding their hair and men bend low holding the women's shoulders against their chests. I run too, finally. I say finally because I do like a good storm. I would be one of those people on the weather channel leaning into the wind while lawmen shout in megaphones: "Get moving!"

Maybe that's because I was born in rough weather. A morning fishermen and wild parrots knew right away was bad news. My mother, limp as a rag waiting for this overdue baby, said she suddenly perked up and decided to hang laundry. Only later did she realize she was drunk with the pure oxygen that swept in before the storm. Halfway through her basket she saw the day turn black, and I began to thrash. She called my father and the two of them delivered me in a downpour. You could say going from womb water straight into rain marked me. It's noteworthy, I suppose, that the first time I saw Mr. Cosey, he was standing in the sea, holding Julia, his wife, in his arms. I was five; he was twenty-four and I'd never seen anything like that. Her eyes were closed, head bobbing; her light blue swimming dress ballooned or flattened out depending on the waves and his strength. She lifted an arm, touched his shoulder. He turned her to his chest and carried her ashore. I believed then it was the sunlight that brought those tears to my eyes—not the sight of all that tenderness coming out of the sea. Nine years later, when I heard he was looking for house help, I ran all the way to his door.

The sign outside reads "Maceo's Cafe——ria" but the diner really belonged to me. Indeed if not in deed. I had been cooking for Bill Cosey close to fifty years when he died, and his funeral flowers were still fresh when I turned my back on his women. I'd done all I could for them; it was time to quit. Rather than starve, I took in laundry so I wouldn't have to. But having customers running in and out of my house was too bothersome, so I gave in to Maceo's pleading. He had a certain reputation for fried fish (sooty black and crisp on the outside; flaky tender inside), but his side orders let you down every time. What I do with okra, with sweet potatoes, hopping John, and almost anything you could name would put this generation of takeout brides to shame if they had any—which they don't. Every house had a serious cook in it once; somebody who toasted bread under an oven flame not in an aluminum box; somebody who beat air into batter with a spoon instead of a machine, who knew the secret of cinnamon bread. Now, well, it's all over. People wait for Christmas or Thanksgiving to give their kitchens proper respect. Otherwise they'd come to Maceo's Café Ria and pray I hadn't dropped dead at the stove. I used to walk all the way to work until my feet swole up and I had to quit. A few weeks into daytime TV and my bad health, Maceo knocked on the door and said he couldn't take the empty tables any longer. Said he was willing to drive back and forth between Up Beach and Silk every day if I would save him one more time. I told him it wasn't only the walk; it was standing as well. But he had a plan for that, too. He got me a high chair with wheels so I could scoot from stove to sink to cutting table. My feet healed but I got so used to wheel trans-portation I couldn't give it up.

Anybody who remembers what my real name is is dead or gone and nobody inquires now. Even chil-dren, who have a world of time to waste, treat me like I'm dead and don't ask about me anymore. Some thought it was Louise or Lucille because they used to see me take the usher's pencil and sign my tithe envelopes with L. Others, from hearing people mention or call me, said it was El for Eleanor or Elvira. They're all wrong. Anyway, they gave up. Like they gave up calling Maceo's Maceo's or sup-plying the missing letters. Café Ria is what it's known as, and like a favored customer spoiled by easy transportation, I glide there still.

Girls like the place a lot. Over iced tea with a

clove in it, they join their friends to repeat what he
said, describe what he *did, and guess what* he *meant*
by any of it. Like

He didn't call me for three days and when I
called him he wanted to get together right
then. See there? He wouldn't do that if he
didn't want to be with you. Oh, please. When I
got there we had a long talk and for the first
time he really listened to me. Sure he did. Why
not? All he had to do was wait till you shut up,
then he could work his own tongue. I thought
he was seeing what's her name? No, they split.
He asked me to move in. Sign the paper first,
honey. I don't want anybody but him. It's like
that, huh? Well, no joint accounts, hear? You
want porgies or not?

*Foolish. But they spice the lunch hour and lift
the spirits of brokenhearted men eavesdropping at
nearby tables.*

*We never had waitresses at the diner. The food is
displayed in steam trays, and after your plate is
heaped you take it to the cash register for cost analysis done by Maceo, his wife, or one of his no-count
sons. Then you can eat here or take it on home.*

*The girl with no underwear—she calls herself
Junior—comes in a lot. The first time I saw her she
looked to me like somebody in a motorcycle gang.*

Boots. Leather. Wild hair. Maceo couldn't take his eyes off her either—had to lid her coffee twice. The second time was on a Sunday just before church let out. She walked the length of the steam table checking the trays with the kind of eyes you see on those "Save This Child" commercials. I was resting by the sink and blowing on a cup of pot liquor before dipping my bread in. I could see her pacing like a panther or some such. The big hair was gone. It was done up in a million long plaits with something shiny at the tip of each one. Her fingernails were painted blue and her lipstick was dark as blackberries. She still wore that leather jacket, and her skirt was long this time, but you could see straight through it—a flowery nothing swinging above her boots. All her private parts going public alongside red dahlias and baby's breath.

One of Maceo's trifling boys leaned up against the wall while Miss Junior made up her mind. He never opened his lips to say good afternoon, may I help you? anything in particular? or any of the welcoming things you're supposed to greet customers with. I just cooled my liquid and watched to see which one would behave normal first.

She did.

Her order must have been for herself and a friend, because Christine came back home a champion cook and Heed won't eat. Anyway, the girl chose three sides, two meats, one rice pudding, and one chocolate cake. Maceo's boy, Theo they call him, smirking more than usual, moved from the wall to load up the Styrofoam plates. He let the stewed tomatoes slide over the compartments to discolor the potato salad, and forked the barbecue on top of the gravied chicken. I got so heated watching Theo disrespect food I dropped the bread into my cup, where it fell apart like grits.

She never took her eyes off the trays. Never met Theo's hateful stare until he gave her change at the register. Then she looked right at him and said, "I see why you need a posse. Your dick don't work one on one?"

Theo shouted a nasty word to her back, but it fell flat with no audience but me. Long after the door slammed, he kept on repeating it. Typical. Young people can't waste words because they don't have too many.

When Maceo walked in, ready to take over before the after-church lines started forming, Theo was dribbling air balls in his dream court behind the register. As if he'd just been signed by Orlando and the Wheaties people too. Not a bad way to work off shame. Quick, anyway. Takes some people a lifetime.

This Junior girl—something about her puts me in mind of a local woman I know. Name of Celestial. When she was young, that is, though I doubt if Junior or any of these modern tramps could match her style. Mr. Cosey knew her too, although if you *asked him he'd deny it. Not to me, though. Mr. Cosey never lied to me. No point in it. I knew his first wife better than he did. I knew he adored her and I knew what she began to think of him after she found out where his money came from. Contrary to the tale he put in the street, the father he bragged about had earned his way as a Courthouse informer. The one police could count on to know where a certain colored boy was hiding, who sold liquor, who had an eye on what property, what was said at church meetings, who was agitating to vote, collecting money for a school—all sorts of things Dixie law was interested in. Well paid, tipped off, and favored for fifty-five years, Daniel Robert Cosey kept his evil gray eye on everybody. For the pure power of it, people supposed, because he had no joy, and the money he got for being at the beck and call of white folks in general and police in particular didn't bring comfort to him or his family. Whites called him Danny Boy. But to Negroes his initials, DRC, gave rise to the name he was known by: Dark. He worshiped paper money and coin, withheld decent shoes from his son and passable dresses from his wife and daughters, until he died leaving 114,000 resentful dollars behind. The son decided to enjoy his share. Not throw it away, exactly, but use it on things Dark cursed: good times, good clothes, good food, good music, dancing till the sun came up in a hotel made for it all. The father was dreaded; the son was a ray of* light. The cops paid off the father; the son paid off the cops. What the father corrected, the son celebrated. The father a miser? The son an easy touch. Spendthrift didn't cut ice with Julia. Her family were farmers always being done out of acres by white landowners and spiteful Negroes. She froze when she learned how blood-soaked her husband's money was. But she didn't have to feel ashamed too long. She gave birth and waited a dozen years to see if history skipped a generation or blossomed in her son. I don't know if she was satisfied or just lost interest, because her last whisper was, "Is that my daddy?"

4

BENEFACTOR

Heed eased down into the froth, hanging on to the tub's rim with a practiced use of her thumbs. Once on her knees she could turn, sit, and watch the lilac foam rise to her shoulders.

This can't last, she thought. I'm going to sink or slip and not have the wrist strength to save myself from drowning.

She hoped Junior's list of things she was willing to do—"You want your hair fixed, I'll fix it. You want a bath, I'll give you one"—was honest, not the eager lies of a job hunter. Heed decided to test her on the hairdressing before asking for help with her bath. July was the last time she had been able to hold the Clairol bottle and flood the silver seams at her scalp with Deep Walnut. How, she wondered, how had it happened that she, who had never picked a crab, handled crawfish or conch, ended up with hands more deformed than those of the factory workers who had. Ben-Gay, aloe, Aspercreme did little to help, and constant bathing was needed to stop the sea life she had never touched from touching her. So the first two tasks for Junior would be to color her hair and help in the bath—assuming she could get her attention away from Romen long enough.

She didn't need to know what Junior had said to him. Watching the boy's face from her bedroom window, Heed thought the girl may as well have shouted. His grin, his eyes gone liquid. Soon the two of them would be coiled together right under her nose. In the garage under a quilt. No. Junior was bold. She would sneak him into her bedroom, or some other room. Christine might not like it. Or maybe she wouldn't care. If she was feeling hateful or jealous, she would tear them up. If her slut history reared itself, she might enjoy it. Nobody knew which way the gray-eyed cat would jump. On her ninth life, Lord willing. Heed thought it a good thing, this baby romance, a way to keep the girl on the premises once she found out there was no way to steal. It was enough that Christine was pilfering the household money to pay that lawyer. A little backseat fumbling might loosen up Romen too. Yank him out of Vida's clamp. He was so tight around the mouth. "Yes, ma'am. No, ma'am. No thank you, I have to be home by streetlights." What had Vida and Sandler told him about her? About Christine? Whatever they'd said, it wasn't so awful they didn't want him to work there. Just don't get too familiar, Vida would say. But if Romen had reasons of his own to hang around, he could be more useful than he already was. He had followed her instructions perfectly when she dictated the *Harbor Journal* ad. Junior's thief-smarts would teach him the strut he needed to manage Vida and stop treating everybody old enough to pay taxes as an enemy and old women, in particular, as fools.

Heed was used to that. Depended on it, in fact. Trusting that whoever answered her ad would need money, she'd been lucky that the first and only applicant was slick as well as greedy. They had postured for each other last night, and while Miss Viviane was busy casing the room, Heed was busy casing her; while she was busy taking control, Heed was letting her believe she already had it. Her insight was polished to blazing by a lifetime of being underestimated. Only Papa knew better, had picked her out of all he could have chosen. Knowing she had no schooling, no abilities, no proper raising, he chose her anyway while everybody else thought she could be run over. But here she was and where were they? May in the ground, Christine penniless in the kitchen, L haunting Up Beach. Where they belonged. She had fought them all, won, and was still winning. Her bank account was fatter than ever. Only Vida had done fairly well with her life and that was because of Sandler, who had never mocked or insulted Bill Cosey's wife. He had respected her even when his own wife did not. It was he who came to her asking if she would hire his grandson. Polite. Staying for iced coffee in her bedroom. Vida would never have done that. Not just because she disliked Heed, but also because she was afraid of Christine—as she should be. The knife flashed at Cosey's funeral was real, and rumors of Christine's sloppy life included brawls, arrests, torching cars, and prostitution. There was no telling what a mind trained to gutter life would think of.

It was impossible that no one knew of the fights between them when Christine returned to take up permanent residence. Most were by mouth: quarrels about whether the double C's engraved on the silver was one letter doubled or the pairing of Christine's initials. It could be either, because Cosey had ordered the service after his first marriage but long before his second. They argued about twice-stolen rings and the real point of sticking them under a dead man's fingers. But there were also bruising fights with hands, feet, teeth, and soaring objects. For size and willingness Christine should have been the hands-down winner. With weak hands and no size, Heed should have lost every match. But the results were a tie at the least. For Heed's speed more than compensated for Christine's strength, and her swift cunning—anticipating, protecting, warding off—exhausted her enemy. Once—perhaps twice—a year, they punched, grabbed hair, wrestled, bit, slapped. Never drawing blood, never apologizing, never premeditating, yet drawn annually to pant through an episode that was as much rite as fight. Finally they stopped, moved into acid silence, and invented other ways to underscore bitterness. Along with age, recognition that neither one could leave played a part in their unnegotiated cease-fire. More on the mark was their unspoken realization that the fights did nothing other than allow them to hold each other. Their grievances were too serious for that. Like friendship, hatred needed more than physical intimacy; it wanted creativity and hard work to sustain itself. The first fight, interrupted in 1971, signaled the will to claw each other. It began when Christine stole from Heed's desk the jewelry Papa had won in a card game—a paper bag of engagement rings he agreed to try to fence for a drummer with a police record. Rings Christine pretended she wanted to place in Papa's hands in his coffin. Four years later she pushed her way into Heed's house holding a shopping bag with fingers loaded with that collection of other women's hopes; demanding rights and the space to take care of May, her sick mother—the same mother she had been laughing at for years when she took the trouble to think about her at all. Immediately the postponed fight resumed and remained intermittent for a decade. When they searched for more interesting means of causing pain they had to rely on personal information, things they remembered from childhood. Each thought she was in charge. Christine because she was strappingly healthy, could drive, go about, and run the house. Heed, however, knew she was still in charge, still winning, not only because she had the money but because she was what everybody but Papa assumed she was not: smart. Smarter than the petted one, the spoiled one miseducated in private school, stupid about men, unequipped for real work and too lazy to do it anyway; a parasite feeding off men until they dumped her and sent her home to gnaw the hand she ought to be licking.

Heed was sure she knew Christine better than Christine knew herself. And notwithstanding an acquaintanceship merely twelve hours old, she knew Junior too, and now she knew what the sexpot was thinking: how to fool an arthritic old woman, how to use her to satisfy and hide her cravings. Heed knew all about that too, about cravings sharp enough to bring tears of rage to grown-up eyes. Like May's when she learned who her father-in-law would marry. And young eyes. Like Christine's when she knew her best friend was the chosen one. Both of them, mother and daughter, went wild just thinking about his choice of an Up Beach girl for his bride. A girl without a nightgown or bathing suit. Who had never used two pieces of flatware to eat. Never knew food to be separated on special plates. Who slept on the floor and bathed on Saturday in a washtub full of the murky water left by her sisters. Who might never get rid of the cannery fish smell. Whose family salvaged newsprint not for reading but for the privy. Who could not form a correct sentence; who knew some block letters but not script. Under those cir-

cumstances, she had to be braced every minute
of the day. Papa protected her, but he wasn't
around all the time or in every place where
people could mess with her, because May and
Christine were not the only ones, as a particular afternoon proved. With the necessary
prowess of the semiliterate, Heed had a flawless
memory, and like most nonreaders, she was
highly numerate. She remembered not only
how many gulls had come to feed off a jelly-
fish but the patterns of their flight when disturbed. Money she grasped completely. In
addition she had hearing as sharp and powerful
as the blind.

The afternoon sizzled. She sat in the gazebo
eating a light lunch. Green salad, ice water.
Thirty yards away, a group of women lolled in
the shade of the porch drinking rum punch.
Two were actresses, one of whom had audi-
tioned for *Anna Lucasta;* two were singers; the
other one studied with Katherine Dunham.
Their conversation wasn't loud, but Heed
caught every word of it.

How could he marry her? Protection. From
what? Other women. I don't think so. Does he
play around? Probably. Are you crazy, sure he
does. She's not bad-looking. Good figure. Way
past good; she could be in the Cotton Club.
Except for her color. And she'd have to smile

some of the time. Needs to do something with her hair. Tell me about it. So, why, why'd he pick her? Beats me. She's hard to be around. Hard how? I don't know; she's sort of physical. (Long laughter.) Meaning? You know, jungle-y. (Choking laughter.)

While they talked, four rivulets coursed down the side of Heed's glass, breaking paths through moisture. Pimento eyes bulged in their olive sockets. Lying on a ring of onion, a tomato slice exposed its seedy smile, one she remembers to this moment.

Papa insisted she learn how to run the hotel and she did learn, despite local sniggering and May and Christine's sabotage. They smoldered in an outrage kept lit by the radiance the couple brought with them to breakfast and their anticipatory glow at supper. Thoughts of Papa and her together in bed drove the two of them to more and newer meanness. The war had already been declared on the wedding gown Papa had ordered from Texas. Expensive, beautiful, it was way too big. L pinned it for alteration, but the gown could not be found until the afternoon of the ceremony, when it was too late. L folded the cuffs, safety-pinned the hem, still it took a lot for Heed to grin her way down the stairs into the hotel lobby and through the ceremony. A ceremony unob-

served by Heed's own family because, other
than Solitude and Righteous Morning, none
of her family was allowed to attend. The given
excuse was that they were still mourning the
deaths of Joy and Welcome. The real reason
was May, who took pains to snub the whole
Johnson brood. She even objected to Papa's
paying for the funerals—muttering that the
boys had no business swimming in "their" part
of the ocean. Only Heed's younger sisters were
permitted to squeeze into the room and listen
to "Oh Promise Me." From that spitefulness
May and her daughter moved on to relentless
criticism of the young bride: her speech,
hygiene, table manners, and thousands of things
Heed didn't know. What "endorse a check"
meant; how to dress a bed; how to dispose of
sanitary napkins; how to set a table; how to
estimate supplies. She could have learned to
read script if that deficiency had not been a
running joke. L, who liked her in those days,
taught her a lot and saved the life Papa had
given her and her alone. She could never have
navigated those treacherous waters if L hadn't
been the current. Heed had not thought much
about it at the time, but she took it for granted
that her husband would be generous with her.
He had already paid for her brothers' funerals;
gave her mother a present and put a grateful

smile on her father's face. She had no idea that so many other people—especially her own family—waited to take advantage of him. Her kinfolk so overreached, they forced the break that was never repaired. As soon as the wedding was over, they crept up on her. Hinting— "I heard they're hiring but you need work shoes to get taken ..." "Did you see that dress Lola gave her mama? ..." Begging—"Ask him if he can lend me a little till ..." "You know I'm short since ..." "I'll pay you all back as soon as ..." Demanding—"Bring me some a that ..." "Is this all?" "You don't need that, do you?" By the time they were told to stay off hotel property, Heed was too ashamed to object. Even Righteous and Solitude began to wonder about her loyalty. Recriminations and accusations peppered her visits to Up Beach, and when she told Papa why her eyes were puffy, she was relieved by his firm response. All she needed was him, which was lucky because he was all she had.

Up to her neck in lilac bubbles, Heed rested her head on the tub's curve of porcelain. Stretching, she manipulated the chain with her toe to pull out the stopper, then waited until the water drained. If she slipped and knocked herself out, at least she had a chance of coming to without drowning.

This is dumb as well as dangerous, she thought, climbing out of the tub. I can't do it no more.

Wrapped in a towel, resting in Papa's red barber's chair, she decided to ask—no, order—Junior to help her right away in and out of the tub. It was a necessary sacrifice she did not look forward to. Dependency, awkwardness while exposing her poor soft nakedness to the judging glance of a firm young girl did not matter. What troubled Heed, had made her hesitate, was the loss of skin memory, the body's recollection of pleasure. Of her wedding night, for instance, submerged in water in his arms. Creeping away from the uncomfortable reception, out the back door into the dark, rushing in tuxedo and way-too-big bridal gown across sea grass to powdery sand. Undressing. No penetration. No blood. No eeks of pain or discomfort. Just this man stroking, nursing, bathing her. She arched. He stood behind her, placed his hands behind her knees, and opened her legs to the surf. Skin might forget that in the company of a sassy girl whose flesh was accumulating its own sexual memories like tattoos. The latest of which, apparently, would be Romen's mark. Where would it go? What would it look like? Junior probably had so many it would be hard to find space. They would merge finally into a lacy net covering her whole body, making indistinguishable one image from another; one boy from another.

Heed's own story was dyed in colors restored to their original clarity in bubbly water. She would have to figure out a way to prevent Junior's presence from erasing what her skin knew first in seafoam.

Once a little girl wandered too far—down to big water and along its edge where waves skidded and mud turned into clean sand. Ocean spray dampened the man's undershirt she wore. There on a red blanket another little girl with white ribbons in her hair sat eating ice cream. The water was very blue. Beyond, a crowd of people laughed. "Hi, want some?" asked the girl, holding out a spoon.

They ate ice cream with peaches in it until a smiling woman came and said, "Go away now. This is private."

Later, making footprints in the mud, she heard the ice cream girl call, "Wait! Wait!"

The kitchen was big and shiny, full of grown people busy cooking, talking, banging pots. The one who had said "Go away" smiled even more and the ice cream girl was her friend.

Heed put on a fresh nightgown and an old-fashioned satin robe. At a dressing table she studied her face in the mirror.

"Go away?" she asked her reflection. "Wait?" How could she do both? They tried to chase her from white sand back to mud, to stop her with a hidden wedding gown, but in time the one who shouted "Wait!" was gone and the one who said "Go away" was shunned. Spoiled silly by the wealth of an openhanded man, they hadn't learned, or had learned too late. Even now she knew that any interested folk would think her life was that of an idle old lady reduced to poring over papers, listening to the radio, and bathing three times a day. They didn't understand that winning took more than patience; it took a brain. A brain that did not acknowledge a woman who could summon your husband anytime she wanted to. Whose name he kept secret even in his sleep. Oh girl. Oh girl. Let him moan; let him "go fishing" without tackle or bait. There were remedies. But now there was less time.

Christine knew it and had suddenly driven off to consult with her lawyer. One of those so-called new professional black women with twenty years of learning that Christine hoped could outwit a woman who had bested an entire town: defeated her daughter-in-law, run Christine off, and raised herself above all those

conniving folks begging favors who, no matter
what she did, still threw up behind her back.
For as long as she could remember, Heed
believed stomachs turned in her company.
Truth be told, Papa was the only person who
did not make her feel that way. She was safe
with him no matter what he muttered in his
sleep. And there was no question about what
he meant her to have when he died. Will or
none, nobody would ever believe he preferred
Christine, whom he hadn't seen since 1947, to
his own wife. Unless it was one of those
lawyer-type black girls, full of themselves,
despising women of Heed's generation who
had more business sense in their tooth fill-
ings than those educated half-wits would ever
know.

Since there was nothing else, the notes for a
will that L found scribbled on a menu were
legal, provided no other, later, and contra-
dictory writing could be found. Provided.
Provided. Suppose, however, later writing, sup-
porting, clarifying the first was found. Not a
real notarized will—there was none, and if
there ever was one, crazy May had hidden it, as
she had the deed—but another menu from a
year after the 1958 one, one that actually iden-
tified the deceased's "sweet Cosey child" by
name: Heed Cosey. If Papa jotted down his

wishes in 1958 and again on whatever subsequent menu Heed could find, no judge would favor Christine's appeal.

It was not a new thought. Heed had mused about such a miracle for a very long time; since 1975, when Christine had pushed her way into the house flashing diamonds and claiming it as hers. What was new, recent, was the jolt to Heed's memory last summer. Lotioning her hands, trying to flex her fingers, move them apart, examining the familiar scar tissue on the back of her hand, Heed revisited the scene of the accident. Muggy kitchen, worktable stacked with cartons. Electric knife, Sunbeam mixer, General Electric toaster oven—all brand-new. L wordlessly refusing to open them, let alone use the equipment they contained. 1964? 1965? Heed is arguing with L. May enters the kitchen with her own cardboard box, wearing that stupid army hat. She is carrying an institutional-size carton that once held boxes of Rinso. She is frantic with worry that the hotel and everybody in it are in immediate danger. That city blacks have already invaded Up Beach, carrying lighter fluid, matches, Molotov cocktails; shouting, urging the locals to burn Cosey's Hotel and Resort to the ground and put the Uncle Toms, the sheriff's pal, the race traitor out of business.

Papa said the protesters had no idea of what real betrayal was; that May should have married his father, not his son. Without a dot of proof, a hint of attack, threat, or even disrespect except the mold growing in her own mind, May was beyond discussion, assigning herself the part of the resort's sole protector.

Once she had been merely another of the loud defenders of colored-owned businesses, the benefits of separate schools, hospitals with Negro wards and doctors, colored-owned banks, and the proud professions designed to service the race. Then she discovered that her convictions were no longer old-time racial uplift, but separatist, "nationalistic." Not sweet Booker T., but radical Malcolm X. In confusion she began to stutter, contradict herself. She forced agreement from the like-minded and quarreled endlessly with those who began to wonder about dancing by the sea while children blew apart in Sunday school; about holding up property laws while neighborhoods fell in flames. As the Movement swelled and funerals, marches, and riots was all the news there was, May, prophesying mass executions, cut herself off from normal people. Even guests who agreed began to avoid her and her warnings of doom. She saw rebellion in the waiters; weapons in the hands of the yard help.

A bass player was the first to publicly shame her. "Aw, woman. Shut the fuck up!" It was not said to her face, but to her back and loud enough to be heard. Other guests became equally blatant, or just got up and left when she entered their company.

Eventually May quieted, but she never changed her mind. She simply went about removing things, hiding them from the kerosene fires she knew were about to be lit any day now. From grenades lobbed and land mines buried in sand. Her reach was both wide and precise. She patrolled the beach and set booby traps behind her bedroom door. She hid legal documents and safety pins. As early as 1955, when a teenager's bashed-up body proved how seriously whites took sass, and sensing disorder when word of an Alabama boycott spread, May recognized one fortress—the hotel—and buried its deed in the sand. Ten years later, the hotel's clientele, short-tempered and loud, treated her with the courtesy you'd give a stump. And when waves of Blacks crashed through quiet neighborhoods as well as business districts, she added the Monarch Street house to her care. Controlling nothing in either place, she went underground, locking away, storing up. Money and silverware nestled in sacks of Uncle Ben's rice; fine table linen hid toilet paper and toothpaste; tree holes were stuffed with emergency underwear; photographs, keepsakes, mementos, junk she bagged, boxed, and squirreled away.

Panting, she comes into the hotel kitchen carrying her loot while Heed argues about the waste L is causing by her refusal to open the cartons, use the equipment, and thereby produce more meals faster. L never looks up, just keeps dredging chicken parts in egg batter, then flour. An arc of hot fat escapes the fryer, splashes Heed's hand.

Until recently that was all she remembered of the scene—the burn. Thirty years later, lotioning her hands, she remembered more. Before the pop of hot fat. Stopping May, checking the Rinso box, seeing useless packets of last New Year's cocktail napkins, swizzle sticks, paper hats, and a stack of menus. Hearing her say, "I have to put these away." That afternoon the new equipment disappeared, to be found later in the attic—L's final, wordless comment. Now Heed was convinced that May's particular box of junk was still there—in the attic. Fifty menus must have been in it. Prepared weekly, daily, or monthly, depending on L's whims, each menu had a date signaling the freshness of the food, its home-cooked accuracy. If the fat hit her hand in 1964 or '65, when May, reacting in terror to Mississippi or Watts, had to be followed to retrieve needed items, then the menus she was storing were prepared seven years later than the 1958 one accepted as Bill Cosey's only will and testament. There would be a lot of untampered-with menus in that box. Only one was needed. That, a larcenous heart, and a young, steady hand that could write script.

Good old May. Years of cunning, decades of crazy—both equaled the simplemindedness that might just save the day. If she were alive it would kill her. Before her real death she was already a minstrel-show spook, floating through the rooms, flapping over the grounds, hiding behind doors until it was safe to bury evidence of a life the Revolution wanted to deprive her of. Yet she might rest easy now, since when she died in 1976, her beloved death penalty was back in style and she had outlived the Revolution. Her ghost, though, helmeted and holstered, was alive and gaining strength.

An orange-scented road to Harbor was what Christine expected, because three times the aroma had accompanied her escapes. The first was on foot, the second by bus, and each time the orange trees lining the road marked her flight with a light citric perfume. More than familiar, the road formed the structure of her dreamlife. From silly to frightening, every memorable dream she had took place on or near Route 12, and if not visible, the road lurked just beyond the dreaming, ready to assist a scary one or provide the setting for the incoherent happiness of a sweet dream. Now, as she pressed the gas pedal, her haste certainly had the feel of a nightmare—panting urgency in stationary time—but freezing weather had killed the young fruit along with its fragrance and Christine was keenly aware of the absence. She rolled the window down, then up, then down again.

Romen's version of washing the car did not include opening its doors, so the Oldsmobile sparkled on the outside while its interior smelled like a holding cell. She once fought a better class of car than this because of an odor. Tried to kill it and everything it stood for, but trying mostly to kill the White Shoulders stinging her sinuses and clotting her tongue. The owner, Dr. Rio, never saw the damage because his new girlfriend had the car towed away before the sight of it could break his heart. So Christine's hammer swings against the windshield, the razor cuts through plump leather; the ribbons of tape (including and especially Al Green's "For the Good Times") that she draped over the dashboard and steering wheel he only heard about, never saw. And that hurt as much as his dismissal had. Killing a Cadillac was never easy, but doing it in bright daylight in the frenzy of another woman's cologne was an accomplishment that deserved serious witnessing by the person for whom it was meant. Dr. Rio was spared, according to Christine's landlady, by his new woman. A mistake, Manila had said. The new woman should have let him learn the lesson—observe the warning of what a displaced woman could do. If he had been allowed to see the result of getting rid of one woman, it might help the new one convert her own rental in his arms to a longer lease.

Regrets over her mismanaged life faded in the glow of Dr. Rio's memory, as did the embarrassment of her battle with his beloved Cadillac. In spite of the shamefaced end of their affair, the three years with him—well, near him; he was mightily undivorceable— were wonderful. She had seen movies about the misery of kept women, how they died in the end or had suffering illegitimate babies who died also. Sometimes the women were saddened by guilt and cried on the betrayed wife's lap. Yet twenty years after she'd been replaced by fresher White Shoulders, Christine still insisted her kept-woman years were the best. When she met Dr. Rio, her forty-one years to his sixty made him an "older" man. Now, in her mid-sixties, the word meant nothing. He was sure to be dead by now or propped up in bed paying some teenage welfare mother a hundred dollars to nibble his toes while a day nurse monitored his oxygen flow. It was a scene she had to work at because the last sight she'd had of him was as seductive as the first. An elegant dresser, successful G.P., passionate, playful. Her last good chance for happiness wrecked by the second oldest enemy in the world: another woman. Manila's girls said Dr. Rio gave each new mistress a gift of that same cologne. Christine had thought it was unique—a private gesture from a thoughtful suitor. He preferred it; she learned to. Had she stayed longer at Manila's or visited her whores once in a while, she would have discovered at once Dr. Rio's particular pattern of bullshit: he fell head over heels, seduced, offered his expensive apartment on Trelaine Avenue, and sent dracaena and White Shoulders on the day the replacement moved in. Unlike roses or other cut flowers, dracaena was meant to speak legitimacy, permanence. The

White Shoulders—who knew? Maybe he read about it somewhere, in a men's magazine invented to show men the difference between suave and a shampoo. Some creaky, unhip glossy for teenagers disguised as men that catalogued seduction techniques, as if any technique at all was needed when a woman decided on a man. He could have sent a bottle of Clorox and a dead Christmas tree—she would have done whatever he wanted for what he made available. Complete freedom, total care, reliable sex, reckless gifts. Trips, short and secret lest his wife find out, parties, edginess, and a satisfactory place in the pecking order of a certain middle-class black society that understood itself to swing, if the professional credentials and money were right.

Route 12 was empty, distracting Christine from the urgency of her mission with scattered recollections of the past. How abrupt the expulsion from first-class cabins on romantic cruises to being head-pressed into a patrol car; from a coveted table at an NMA banquet to rocking between her own elbows on a hooker's mattress aired daily to rid it of the previous visitors' stench. When she went back to Manila's, dependent on her immediate but short-lived generosity, Christine poured the remains of her own White Shoulders down the toilet and packed her shoes, pride, halter top, brassiere, and pedal pushers into a shopping bag. Everything but the diamonds and her silver spoon. Those she zipped into her purse along with Manila's loan of fifty dollars. Manila's girls had been congenial most of the time; other times not. But they so enjoyed their hearts of gold—gold they had slipped from wallets, or inveigled with mild forms of blackmail—they were staunchly optimistic. They told Christine not to worry, some woman was bound to de-dick him one day, and besides, she was still a fox, there were lots of players and every goodbye ain't gone. Christine appreciated their optimism but was not cheered. Thrown out of the apartment after she had refused for weeks to leave quietly; prevented from taking her furs, suede coat, leather pants, linen suits, the Saint Laurent shoes—even her diaphragm: this goodbye was final. The four Samsonite suitcases she had left home with in 1947 held all she thought she would ever need. In 1975 the Wal-Mart shopping bag she returned with contained all she owned. Considering how much practice she had had, her exits from Silk should not have become more and more pitiful. The first one as a thirteen-year-old, the result of a temper tantrum, failed in eight hours; the second one at seventeen, a run for her life, was equally disastrous. Both escapes were fed by malice, but the third and last, in 1971, was a calm attempt to avert the slaughter she had in mind. Leaving other places: Harbor, Jackson, Grafenwöhr, Tampa, Waycross, Boston, Chattanooga—or any of the towns that once beckoned—was easy until Dr. Rio had her forcibly evicted for no good reason she could think of except a wish for fresh dracaena or a younger model for the furs he passed along from one mistress to another. Following days of reflection at Manila's (named for a father's heroic exploits), Christine discovered a way to convert a return to Silk in shame and on borrowed money into an act of filial responsibility: taking care of her ailing mother, and a noble battle for justice—her lawful share of the Cosey estate.

She remembered the bus ride back, punctured by drifts of sleep flavored with sea salt. With one explosive exception (during which fury blinded her), it was her first glimpse of Silk in twenty-eight years. Neat houses stood on streets named for heroes and the trees destroyed to build them. Maceo's was still on Gladiator across from Lamb of God, holding its own against a new hamburger place on Prince Arthur called Patty's. Then home: a familiar place that, when you left, kept changing behind your back. The creamy oil painting you carried in your head turned into house paint. Vibrant, magical neighbors became misty outlines of themselves. The house nailed down in your dreams and nightmares comes undone, not sparkling but shabby, yet even more desirable because what had happened to it had happened to you. The house had not shrunk; you had. The windows were not askew—you were. Which is to say it was more yours than ever.

Heed's look, cold and long, had been anything but inviting, so Christine just slammed past her through the door. With very few words they came to an agreement of sorts because May was hopeless, the place filthy, Heed's arthritis was disabling her hands, and because nobody in town could stand them. So the one who had attended private school kept house while the one who could barely read ruled it. The one who had been sold by a man battled the one who had been bought by one. The level of desperation it took to force her way in was high, for she was returning to a house whose owner was willing to burn it down just to keep her out. Had once, in fact, set fire to Christine's bed for precisely that purpose. So this time, for safety she settled in the little apartment next to the kitchen. Some relief surfaced when she saw Heed's useless hands, but knowing what the woman was capable of still caused her heart to beat raggedly in Heed's presence. No one was slyer or more vindictive. So the door between the kitchen and Christine's rooms had a hidden key and a very strong lock.

Christine braked for a turtle crossing the road, but swerving right to avoid it, she drove over a second one trailing the first. She stopped and looked in the rearview mirrors— left one, right one, and overhead—for a sign of life or death: legs pleading skyward for help or a cracked immobile shell. Her hands were shaking. Seeing nothing, she left the driver's seat and ran back down the road. The pavement was blank, the orange trees still. No turtle anywhere. Had she imagined it, the second turtle? The one left behind, Miss Second Best, crushed by a tire gone off track, swerving to save its preferred sister? Scanning the road, she did not wonder what the matter was; did not ask herself why her heart was sitting up for a turtle creeping along Route 12. She saw a movement on the south side of the road where the first turtle had been heading. Slowly she approached and was relieved to see two shiny green shells edging toward the trees. The wheels had missed Miss Second Best, and while the driver was shuddering in the car, she had caught up to the faster one. Transfixed, Christine watched the pair disappear, returning to her car only when another slowed behind it. As she left the verge, the driver smiled, "Ain't you got no toilet at home?"

"Go around, motherfucker!"

He gave her a thick finger and pulled away.

The lawyer might be surprised—Christine had no appointment—but would see her anyway. Each time she forced herself into the office, Christine had been accommodated. Her slide from spoiled girl child to tarnished homelessness had been neither slow nor hidden. Everybody knew. There was no homecoming for her in elegant auto driven by successful husband. No degree-in-hand-with-happy-family-in-tow return. Certainly no fascinating stories about the difficulty of running one's own business or the limitations placed on one's time by demanding executives, clients, patients, agents, or trainers. In short, no hometown sweep full of hints of personal fulfillment and veiled condescension. She was a flop. Disreputable. But she was also a Cosey, and in Harbor the name still lifted eyelids. William Cosey, onetime owner of many houses, a hotel resort, two boats, and a bankful of gossiped-about, legendary cash, always fascinated people, but he had driven the county to fever when they learned he had left no will. Just doodles on a 1958 menu outlining his whiskey-driven desires. Which turned out to be (1) *Julia II* to Dr. Ralph, (2) Montenegro Coronas to Chief Silk, (3) the hotel to Billy Boy's wife, (4) the Monarch Street house and "whatever nickels are left" to "my sweet Cosey child," (5) his '55 convertible to L, (6) his stickpins to Meal Daddy, and on and on down to his record collection to Dumb Tommy, "the best blues guitar player on God's earth." Feeling good, no doubt, from Wild Turkey straight, he had sat down one night with some boozy friends and scrawled among side orders and the day's specials, appetizers, main courses, and desserts the distribution of his wealth to those who pleased him most. Three years after his death a few boozy friends were located and verified the event, the handwriting, and the clarity of the mind that seemed to have had no further thoughts on the matter. Questions flared like snake cowls: Why was he giving Dr. Ralph his newest boat? What Coronas? Chief Buddy's been dead for years, so does his son get them? Boss Silk don't smoke and who is Meal Daddy? The lead singer of the Purple Tones, said Heed. No, the manager of the Fifth

Street Strutters, said May, but he's in prison, can inmates receive bequests? They're just records, fool, he didn't identify you by name, so what? he didn't mention you at all! and why give a convertible to somebody who can't drive you don't need to drive a car to sell it this ain't a will it's a comic book! They focused on stickpins, cigars, and the current value of old 78s—never asking the central question, who was "my sweet Cosey child"? Heed's claim was strong—especially since she called her husband Papa. Yet since, biologically speaking, Christine was the only "child" left, her claim of blood was equal to Heed's claim as widow. Or so she and May thought. But years of absence, no history of working at the hotel except for one summer as a minor, weakened Christine's position. With a certain amusement, the court examined the greasy menu, lingering lazily perhaps over the pineapple-flavored slaw and Fats' Mean Chili, listened to three lawyers, and tentatively (until further evidence could be provided) judged Heed the "sweet Cosey child" of a drunken man's vocabulary.

Gwendolyn East, Attorney-at-Law, thought otherwise, however, and recently she'd told Christine grounds for reversal on appeal were promising. In any case, she said there was room for review, even if no mitigating evidence was found. For years Christine had searched for such evidence—the hotel, the house—and found nothing (except rubbishy traces of May's lunacy). If there was anything else—a real, typed-up intelligible will—it would be in one of Heed's many locked desks behind her bedroom door, also locked nightly against "intruders." Now the matter was urgent. No more waiting for the other to die or, at a minimum, suffer a debilitating stroke. Now a third element was in the mix. Heed had hired a girl. To help write her memoirs, Junior Viviane had said that morning at breakfast. Christine sputtered her coffee at the thought of the word "write" connected with someone who had gone to school off and on for less than five years. Scooping grapefruit sections, Junior had grinned while pronouncing "memoirs" just the way illiterate Heed would have. "Of her family," said Junior. What family, Christine wondered. That nest of beach rats who bathed in a barrel and slept in their clothes? Or is she claiming Cosey blood along with Cosey land?

After mulling over what the girl had told her, Christine had retreated to her apartment—two rooms and a bath annexed to the kitchen, servant's quarters where L used to stay. Unlike the memory-and-junk-jammed rest of the house, the uncluttered quiet there was soothing. Except for pots of plants rescued from violent weather, the apartment looked much the same as it had some fifty years ago when she hid there under L's bed. Misting begonia leaves, Christine found herself unable to decide on a new line of action, so she decided to consult her lawyer. She waited until Romen was due and Junior out of sight on the third floor. Earlier, at breakfast, dressed in clothes Heed must have loaned her (a red suit not seen in public since the Korean War), Junior had looked like a Sunday migrant. Except for the boots, last night's leather was gone, as was the street-life smell she had brought into the house. When Christine saw Romen puttering around in the sunshine, inspecting ice damage done to the shrubs, she called him to help her with the garage door still stuck in ice, then told him to wash the car. When he was done, she drove off, picking up speed as quickly as she could to get to Gwendolyn East before the lawyer's office closed.

Christine's entanglements with the law were varied enough to convince her that Gwendolyn was not to be trusted. The lawyer may know the courts but she didn't know anything about police—the help or the damage they could do long before you saw a lawyer.

The police who had led her away from the mutilated Cadillac were, like Chief Buddy Silk, gentle, respectful, as though her violence was not merely understandable but justified. They handled her like a woman who had assaulted a child molester rather than a car. Her hands were cuffed in front, not behind her back—and loosely. As she sat in the patrol car, the sergeant offered her a lit cigarette and removed a shard of headlight glass from her hair. Neither officer pinched her nipples or suggested what a blow job could do for racial justice. The one time she had been in a killing frame of mind with a hammer instead of a switchblade in her hand, they treated her like a white woman. During four previous arrests— for incendiary acts, inciting mayhem, obstructing traffic, and resisting arrest—she had nothing lethal in her hand and was treated like sewage.

Come to think of it, every serious affair she'd had led straight to jail. First Ernie Holder, whom she married at seventeen, got them both arrested at an illegal social club. Then Fruit, whose pamphlets she passed out and with whom she had lived the longest, got her thirty days, no suspension, for inciting mayhem. Other affairs had overflowed and ended in dramas the law had precise names for: cursing meant assaulting an officer; yanking your arms when cuffed meant resisting arrest; throwing a cigarette too close to a police car meant conspiracy to commit arson; running across the street to get out of the way of mounted police meant obstructing traffic. Finally Dr. Rio. A Cadillac. A hammer. A gentle, almost reluctant arrest. After an hour's wait, no charges pressed, no write-up or interview, they gave her back the shopping bag and let her go.

Go where? she wondered, slinking down the street. She had been manhandled out of her (his) apartment after a two-minute supervised reprieve to get her purse. No clothing can leave the premises, they said, but she was allowed to take some underwear and her cosmetics bag, which, unknown to the lawyer-paid thugs, included a spoon and twelve diamond rings. Aside from the rings she would die rather than pawn, she had a recently canceled MasterCard and seven dollars plus change. She was as lonely as a twelve-year-old watching waves suck away her sand castle. None of her close friends would risk Dr. Rio's displeasure; the not so close ones were chuckling over her fall. So she walked to Manila's and persuaded her to take her in. For just a few days. For free. It was a risky, even impudent request, since Manila did not run a whore-house, as certain sanctimonious people described her home. She simply rented rooms to needy women. The forlorn, the abandoned, those in transit. That these women had regular visitors or remained in transit for years was not Manila's concern.

Christine had all of these requisites in 1947. The bus driver who directed her to 187 Second Street, "right near the glass factory, look for a pink door," either misunderstood or understood completely. She had asked him if he knew of a rooming house and he had given her Manila's address. Despite the difference between her white gloves, little beanie hat, quiet pearls, and a flawless Peter Pan collar and the costumes of Manila's girls, her desperation was equal to theirs. When she stepped out of the taxi it was nine-thirty in the morning. The house seemed ideal. Quiet. Neat. Manila smiled at the four suitcases and said, "Come on in." She explained the rates, the house rules, and the policy on visitors. It was lunchtime before Christine figured out that the visitors were clientele.

She was surprised by how faint her shock was. Her plan was to find secretarial work or, even better, some high-paying postwar work in a factory. Fresh from an overdue sixteenth-birthday party and graduation from Maple Valley, she had landed in a place her mother would have called "a stinking brothel" (as in "Is he going to turn this place into a . . ."). Christine had laughed. Nervously. This is Celestial territory, she thought, remembering a scar-faced woman on the beach. The girls sauntered through the dining room to the living room where Christine sat and, scanning her clothes, spoke among themselves but not to her. It reminded her of her reception at Maple Valley: the cool but thorough examination; the tentative, smoothly hostile questions. When a few of Manila's girls did engage her— "Where you from? Cute hat. Sharp shoes too, where'd you get 'em? Pretty hair"—the similarity increased. The youngest ones talked about their looks, their boyfriends; the older ones gave bitter advice about both. As in Maple Valley, everyone had a role and a matron ruled the stage. She hadn't escaped from anything. Maple Valley, Cosey's Hotel, Manila's whorehouse—all three floated in sexual tension and resentment; all three insisted on confinement; in all three status was money. And all were organized around the pressing needs of men. Christine's second escape, initiated by a home life turned dangerous, was fed by a dream of privacy, of independence. She wanted to make the rules, choose her friends, earn and control her own money. For those reasons alone she believed she would never have stayed at Manila's, but she will never know because, being a colored girl in the 1940s with an education that suited her for nothing but wifehood, it was easy as pie for Ernie Holder to claim her that very night. So long, independence; so long, privacy. He took her out of there into an organization with the least privacy, the most rules, and the fewest choices: the biggest, totally male entity in the world.

Pfc. Ernest Holder had come to Manila's looking to buy some fun and found instead a beautiful girl in a navy suit and pearls reading *Life* magazine on a sofa. Christine accepted his invitation to dinner. By dessert they had plans. Desire so instant it felt like fate. As couplehood goes, it had its moments. As marriage goes, it was ridiculous.

Christine parked and pulled down the visor's mirror to see if she was presentable. It was a move she was not accustomed to, but one she made because of an encounter on her first visit to Gwendolyn East's office. About to enter the building, she had felt a tap on her shoulder. A woman in a baseball cap and tracksuit grinned up at her.

"Ain't you Christine Cosey?"

"I am."

"I thought that was you. I used to work at Cosey's. Way, way back."

"Is that so?"

"I remember you. Best legs on the beach. My, you used to be so cute. Your skin, your pretty hair. I see you still got those eyes, though. Lord, you was one foxy thing. You don't mind me saying that, do you?"

"Of course not," said Christine. "Ugly women know everything about beauty. They have to."

She didn't look back to see if the woman spit or laughed. Yet on each subsequent visit to the lawyer's office, she couldn't stop herself from checking the mirror. The "pretty hair" needed a cut and a style—any style. The skin was still unlined, but "those eyes," looking out, never inward, seemed to belong to somebody else.

Gwendolyn East was not pleased. The whole point of an office was scheduled appointments. Christine's entrance had been like a break-in.

"We have to move," said Christine, pulling the chair closer to the desk. "Something's going on."

"I beg your pardon?" Gwendolyn asked.

"This will business. She has to be stopped."

Gwendolyn decided that encouraging this rough client was not worth the so far non-forthcoming settlement fee. "Listen, Christine. I support you, you know that, and a judge might also. But you *are* living there, rent free, no expenses. The fact is, it could be said that Mrs. Cosey is taking care of you when she is under no obligation to do so. And the benefit of being awarded the property is, in a way, already yours in a manner of speaking. Better, maybe."

"What are you saying? She could put me out on the street any day if she wants to."

"I know," Gwendolyn replied, "but in twenty years she hasn't. What do you make of that?"

"Slavery is what I make of it."

"Come on, Christine." Gwendolyn frowned. "You're not in a rest home or on welfare . . ."

"Welfare? Welfare!" Christine whispered the word at first, then shouted it. "Look. If she dies who gets the house?"

"Whomever she designates."

"Like a brother or a nephew or a cousin or a hospital, right?"

"Whomever."

"Not necessarily to me, right?"

"Only if she wills it."

"No point in killing her then?"

"Christine. You are too funny."

"You listen to me. She's just now hired somebody. A girl. A young girl. She doesn't need me anymore."

"Well." Gwendolyn was thoughtful. "Do you think she would agree to a kind of lease agreement? Something that guarantees you a place there for life and support at some level in return for . . . services?"

Christine threw her head back and scanned the ceiling as though searching for a new language to make herself understood. What to say to this lawyer woman shouldn't be all that hard. After all, Miss East had Up Beach history, was the granddaughter of a cannery girl who suffered a stroke. Slowly she tapped her middle finger on the lawyer's desk to stress certain words. "I am the last, the only, blood relative of William Cosey. For free I have taken care of his house and his widow for twenty years. I have cooked, cleaned, washed her underwear, laundered her sheets, done the shopping . . ."

"I know."

"You don't know! You don't! She is replacing me."

"Wait now."

"She is! That's been her whole life, don't you get it? Replacing me, getting rid of me. I'm always last; all the time the one being told to go, get out."

"Christine, please."

"This is *my* place. I had my sixteenth-birthday party in that house. When I was away at school it was my *address*. It's where I belong and nobody is going to wave some liquor-splashed menu at me and put me out of it!"

"But you were away from the property for years . . ."

"Fuck you! If you don't know the difference between property and a home you need to be kicked in the face, you stupid, you dumb, you cannery trash! You're fired!"

Once there was a little girl with white bows on each of her four plaits. She had a bedroom all to herself beneath the attic in a big hotel. Forget-me-nots dotted the wallpaper. Sometimes she let her brand-new friend stay over and they laughed till they hiccuped under the sheets.

Then one day the little girl's mother came

to tell her she would have to leave her bedroom and sleep in a smaller room on another
floor. When she asked her mother why, she was
told it was for her own protection. There were
things she shouldn't see or hear or know
about.

The little girl ran away. For hours she
walked a road smelling of oranges until a man
with a big round hat and a badge found her
and took her home. There she fought to
reclaim her bedroom. Her mother relented,
but turned the key in the lock to keep her in
the bedroom at night. Soon after, she was sent
away, far away, from things not to be seen,
heard, or known about.

Except for the man wearing a round hat,
and a badge, no one saw her cry. No one ever
has. Even now her "still got those" eyes were
dry. But they were also, for the first time, seeing the treacherous world her mother knew.
She had hated her mother for expelling her
from her bedroom and, when Chief Buddy
brought her back, smacking her face so hard
Christine's chin hit her shoulder. The slap sent
her into hiding under L's bed for two days, so
they sent her away to Maple Valley School,
where she languished for years and where
a mother like May was an embarrassment.
Maple Valley teachers were alarmed by acting-

out Negroes, but they flinched openly when they read May's incoherent letters to the *Atlanta Daily World* about white "honor" and misguided "freedom rides." Christine was happy to confine their relationship to letters she could hide or destroy. Other than a little gossip about famous guests, there was nothing in them of interest to a thirteen-year-old trying to be popular, and as the years passed she didn't even understand them. Christine could laugh at her own ignorance now, but then it was as though May wrote in code: CORE is sitting-in in Chicago (who was she, this Cora?), Mussolini resigned (resigned to what?), Detroit on fire. Did Hitler kill Roosevelt or did Roosevelt kill Hitler—anyway they both died in the same month. Most of the letters, however, were about Heed's doings. Plots, intrigue. Now she finally understood her mother. The world May knew was always crumbling; her place in it never secure. A poor, hungry preacher's child, May saw her life as depending on colored people who rocked boats only at sea. Events begun in 1942 with her father-in-law's second marriage heaped up quickly throughout the war and long after until, disoriented by her struggle against a certain element in her house and beyond it, she became comic. Yet her instincts, thought

Christine, if not her methods, were correct. Her world had been invaded, occupied, turned into scum. Without vigilance and constant protection it slid away from you, left your heart fluttering, temples throbbing, racing down a road that had lost its citrus.

Everyone decided her mother was insane and speculated as to why: widowhood, overwork, no sex, SNCC. It was none of that. Clarity was May's problem. By 1971, when Christine came home for Cosey's funeral, her mother's clarity had been accumulating for years. It had gone from the mild acuteness they called kleptomania to outright brilliance. She covered her bedroom windows with plywood painted red for danger. She lit lookout fires on the beach. Raised havoc with Boss Silk when he refused her purchase of a gun. The sheriff's father, Chief Silk, would have let her, but his son had a different view of Negroes with guns, even though they both wanted to shoot the same people. Now Christine realized that May's understanding of the situation was profound. She had been right in 1971 to sneer at Christine's fake military jacket, Che-style beret, black leotard, miniskirt. Sharp as a tiger's tooth, May instantly recognized the real deal, as was clear from her own attire. People laughed. So what? The army helmet May had taken to wearing was an authentic position and a powerful statement. Even at the funeral, having been encouraged by L to substitute a black scarf, she still carried it under her arm because, contrary to what Christine thought then, it was true that at any minute protection might be needed in the enemy-occupied zone she, and now Christine, lived in. In that zone, readiness was all. Again, Christine felt the sheer bitterness of the past two decades tramping up and down the stairs carrying meals she was too proud to ruin, wading through layers of competing perfumes, trying not to shiver before the "come on" eyes in the painting over that grotesque bed, collecting soiled clothes, washing out the tub, pulling hairs from the drain—if this wasn't hell, it was the lobby.

Heed had long wanted to have May put away, but L's judgment, more restraining than Cosey's, stopped her. When the menu was read for the "will" it was taken to be, and "Billy Boy's wife" was awarded the hotel, Heed shot straight up out of the chair.

"To a nutcase? He leaves our business to a nutcase?"

It got ugly and stayed that way until the lawyer slapped the table, assuring Heed that no one would (could?) stop her from running the hotel. She was needed, and besides her husband had bequeathed her the house, the cash. At which point May, adjusting her helmet, had said, "I beg your damn pardon?"

The argument that followed was a refined version of the ones that had been seething among the women since the beginning: each had been displaced by another; each had a unique claim on Cosey's affection; each had either "saved" him from some disaster or relieved him of an impending one. The only difference about this preburial quarrel was L, whose normal silence seemed glacial then because there was no expression on her face, no listening, no empathy—nothing. Taking advantage of L's apparent indifference, Heed shouted that unstable people should not be allowed to inherit property because they needed "perfessionate" care. Only the arrival of the undertaker, announcing the need for immediate departure to the church, kept Christine's hand from becoming a fist. Temporarily, anyway, because later, at the grave site, seeing Heed's false tears, her exaggerated shuddering shoulders; watching townsfolk treat her as the sole mourner, and the two real Cosey women as unwelcome visitors; angry that her attempt to place the diamonds on Cosey's fingers had been thwarted—Christine exploded. Reaching into her pocket, she leapt toward Heed with a raised arm which L, having suddenly come to life, bent behind her back. "I'll tell," she whispered to one, the other, or to no one in particular. Heed, having thrust her face into Christine's as soon as it was safe, backed off. Nothing L said ever was idle. There were many details of her sorry life that Christine did not want exposed. Dislike she could handle, even ridicule. But not pity. Panicked, she closed the knife and settled for an icy glare. But Heed—why had she obeyed so fast? What was she afraid of? May, however, understood what was needed and immediately took her daughter's side. Stepping forward into that feline heat, she removed Heed's Gone with the Wind hat and tossed it into the air. Perfect. A giggle from somebody opened a space in which Heed chased her hat and Christine cooled.

The tacky display, the selfish disregard for rites due the deceased whom each claimed to honor, angered people, and they said so. What they did not say was how delighted they must have been by the graveside entertainment featuring beret, bonnet, and helmet. Yet in that moment, by tearing Heed's silly hat off, uncrowning the false queen before the world, May became clarity at its most extreme. As it had been when she did everything to separate the two when they were little girls. She had known instinctively the intruder was a snake: penetrating, undermining, sullying, devouring.

According to May's letters, as far back as 1960 Heed had begun to research ways to put her in a rest home or an asylum. But nothing Heed did—not spreading lies, inventing outrages, seeking advice from psychiatric institutions—could force May out. With L watching and without an accomplice, Heed failed. She was forced to put up with the dazzling clarity of the woman who hated her almost as much as Christine did. May's war did not end when Cosey died. She spent her last year watching in ecstasy as Heed's grasping hands turned slowly into wings. Still, Heed's solution to her problems with May had been a good one, and a good idea directed at the wrong person was still good. Besides, L was gone. Hospitals were more hospitable. And now, with a little coaxing, there might just be an accomplice.

Poor Mama. Poor old May. To keep going, to protect what was hers, crazy-like-a-fox was all she could think of. Husband dead; her crumbling hotel ruled by a rabid beach rat, ignored by the man for whom she had slaved, abandoned by her daughter to strange ideas, a running joke to neighbors—she had no place and nothing to command. So she recognized the war declared on her and fought it alone. In bunkers of her own industry. In trenches she dug near watch fires at ocean's edge. A solitary misunderstood intelligence shaping and controlling its own environment. Now she thought of it, Christine's own disorganized past was the result of laziness—emotional laziness. She had always thought of herself as fierce, active, but unlike May, she'd been simply an engine adjusting to whatever gear the driver chose.

No more.

The ocean is my man now. He knows when to rear and hump his back, when to be quiet and simply watch a woman. He can be devious, but he's not a false-hearted man. His soul is deep down there and suffering. I pay attention and know all about him. That kind of understanding can only come from practice, and I had a lot of that with Mr. Cosey. You could say I fathomed his mind. Not right away, of course. I was just a girl when I went to work for him—a married man with a son and a sick wife who needed care every minute of the day and night. He said her name, Julia, so soft you could feel his tenderness as well as his apology. Their son, Billy

Boy, was twelve when Julia Cosey passed, and even though I was only fourteen, it was the most natural thing in the world for me to stay on and look after the two of them. Only a wide heart like his could care that much for a wife and have so much room left over. When Julia Cosey died, Mr. Cosey transferred all of what he felt to his son. Lucky for him, the boy had that insight smart children use with grown-ups in order to stay important. Not by doing what they say, but by figuring out what they really want. A daddy can say "Fend for yourself, boy" when he means "Don't show me up; hurry up and fail." Or he can say "I'll teach you the world," meaning "I'm scared to death of you." I don't know what Mr. Cosey said to his son along those lines, but whatever it was, Billy Boy understood it to mean "Be something I can get up for in the morning; give me something to do while I paddle along." So it didn't matter much if he was a very good son or a really bad one. He only had to be interesting. Just by luck, I suspect, he chose goodness. Mr. Cosey was pleased with everything Billy Boy did and said. He lavished money on him and took him everywhere. With his hair parted in the middle and a cap just like his father's—what a pair they must have been. One getting a trim in the barber's chair, the other one lounging with customers on the bench; sitting in the bleachers at Eagle games, on campstools at sing-out competitions, at narrow tables in country joints where the most gifted musicians played. They slept in rooming houses or just knocked on a door. Mr. Cosey said he wanted Billy Boy to see men enjoy the perfection of their work, so they went to Perdido Street for King Oliver, Memphis for the Tigers, Birmingham for the Barons. They watched how cooks examined market produce, watermen sorted oysters, bartenders, pool-hall rascals, pickpockets, and choirmasters. Everything was a labor lesson from a man proud of his skill. Mr. Cosey said it was life's real education, but it looked to me like truancy from his own father's school. A way to flunk the lessons Dark had taught him.

Besotted attention didn't spoil the boy. He knew his duty and splashed in it, could smile even as his father bragged about him in front of yawning friends. Bragged about his arm with a ball, his cool head in an emergency. How he had extracted a bent nail stuck in a little girl's cheek better than any doctor could have. I saw that one myself. I'd brought the lunch they wanted one day while they wasted time on the beach—knocking pebbles into the sea with baseball bats. Down a ways, a girl, maybe nine or ten years old, was casting into the waves. For what, who knows. Nothing with scales swims this close to the shore. At some point, the wind turned and the home-made fishhook hooked her. Her fingers were dripping red when Billy Boy got to her. He was deft enough and she was grateful, standing there cupping her face without a tear or a moan. But we took her back to the hotel anyway. I sat her in the gazebo, cleaned her cheek, and spread aloe gum and honey on the wound, hoping she was too strong for lockjaw. Over time, as usual, Mr. Cosey plumped up the story. Depending on his mood and his audience, you would have thought the child was about to be dragged into the water by a swordfish if Billy Boy hadn't saved her. Or that he had removed a hook from a little baby's eyeball. Billy smiled at the fat, cherished lies, and took his father's advice in everything, including marriage: to wed a devoted, not calculating, girl. So Billy Boy chose May, who, as anybody could see, would neither disrupt nor rival the bond between father and son. Mr. Cosey was alarmed at first, not being privy to his son's selection, but was made easy when the bride was not only impressed with the hotel but also showed signs of understanding what superior men require. If I was a servant in that place, May was its slave. Her whole life was making sure those Cosey men had what they wanted. The father more than the son; the father more than her own daughter. And what Mr. Cosey, widower, wanted in 1930 should have been impossible. That was the year the whole country began to live on Relief the way Up Beach people did—if they were lucky, that is. If not, they killed themselves or took to the road. Mr. Cosey, however, took advantage. He bought a broke-down "whites only" club at

Sooker Bay from a man honest enough to say that although he swore to God and his pappy he would never sell to niggers, he was happy as a clam to break his vow and take his family away from that bird-infested sidewalk for hurricanes.

Who would have thought that in the teeth of the Depression colored people would want to play, or if they did, how could they pay for it? Mr. Cosey, that's who. Because he knew what a harmonica player on a street corner knew: where there was music there was money. Check the churches if you doubt it. And he believed something else. If colored musicians were treated well, paid well, and coddled, they would tell each other about such a place where they could walk in the front door, not the service entrance; eat in the dining room, not the kitchen; sit with the guests, sleep in beds, not their automobiles, buses, or in a whorehouse across town. A place where their instruments were safe, their drinks unwatered, their talent honored so they didn't have to go to Copenhagen or Paris for praise. Flocks of colored people would pay to be in that atmosphere. Those who had the money would pay it; those who didn't would find it. It comforts everybody to think of all Negroes as dirt poor, and to regard those who were not, who earned good money and kept it, as some kind of shameful miracle. White people liked that idea because Negroes with money and sense made them nervous. Colored people liked it because, in *those days, they trusted poverty, believed it was a virtue and a sure sign of honesty. Too much money had a whiff of evil and somebody else's blood. Mr. Cosey didn't care. He wanted a playground for folk who felt the way he did, who studied ways to contradict history.*

But it had to be special: evening dress in the evening; sport clothes for sport. And no zoot suits. Flowers in the bedrooms, crystal on the table. Music, dancing, and if you wanted to, you could join a private card game where money changed hands among a few friends—musicians, doctors who enjoyed the excitement of losing what most people couldn't earn. Mr. Cosey was in heaven, then. He liked George Raft clothes and gangster cars, but he used his heart like Santa Claus. If a family couldn't pay for a burial, he had a quiet talk with the undertaker. His friendship with the sheriff got many a son out of handcuffs. For years and without a word, he took care of a stroke victim's doctor bills and her granddaughter's college fees. In those days, the devoted outweighed the jealous and the hotel basked in his glow.

May, a sweet-tempered daughter of a preacher, was bred to hard work and duty, and took to the business like a bee to pollen. At first the two of us managed the kitchen, with Billy Boy tending bar. When it became clear that the queen at the stove was me, she moved to housekeeping, bookkeeping, provisioning, and her husband booked the musicians. I think I deserve half the credit for the way the hotel grew. Good food and Fats Waller is a once-in-a-life-time combination. Still, you had to admire May. She was the one who arranged everything, saw to the linen, paid the bills, controlled the help. The two of us were like the back of a clock. Mr. Cosey was its face telling you the time was now.

When we were just the two females, things went along fine. It was when the girls got in the picture—Christine and Heed—that things began to fray. Oh, I know the "reasons" given: cannery smell, civil rights, integration. And May's behavior did go strange in 1955 when that boy from Chicago tried to act like a man and got beat to death for his trouble. Mississippi's answer to desegregation and whatever else that wilted their sex. We all shivered about what they did to that boy. He had such light eyes. But for May it was a sign. It sent her to the beach where she buried not just the deed but a flashlight and Lord knows what else. Any day now some Negro was going to rile waiting whites, give them an excuse to hang somebody and close the hotel down. Mr. Cosey despised her dread. I guess it was too close to home. Having grown up the son of a stooge, he danced all the harder. Whether the place thrived or didn't, the decline started way before 1955. I foresaw it in 1942 when Mr. Cosey was making money hand over fist and the hotel was a showplace. See that window over there? It looked out on paradise, one me and May made, because when Billy Boy died, Mr. Cosey bought the barber chair the two of them used to take turns in and, for a year or so, just sat in it. Then suddenly he revved back up, ordered some fine silverware, and joined us in keeping the hotel the hot spot folks enjoyed. Handsome dog. Even in those days, when men wore hats—and a man in a hat looks so good—he was something to see. Women trailed him everywhere and I kept my eyes open for who he might pick. The hooked C's on the silverware worried me because I thought he took casual women casually. But if doubled C's were meant to mean Celestial Cosey, he was losing his mind. Still, I was knocked out of my socks in 1942 when he did choose. Word was he wanted children, lots of children, to fill the mirror for him the way Billy Boy used to. For motherhood only an unused girl would do. After playing around awhile, Mr. Cosey ended up in the most likely place for making babies and the least likely for a virgin. Up Beach, where every woman's obituary could have read "Death by Children." It was marrying Heed that laid the brickwork for ruination. See, he chose a girl already spoken for. Not promised to anyone by her parents. That trash gave her up like they would a puppy. No. The way I see it, she belonged to Christine and Christine belonged to her. Anyway, if he was hoping to change the blood he once tried to correct, he failed. Heed never gave him a tadpole, and *like most men, he believed the fault was hers. He waited a few years into the marriage before going back to his favorite, but back to Celestial he went. You'd think since one of his women had a stroke after rooting with him in the sand, he'd avoid the beach as a setting for fun. But he didn't. He even spent his wedding night there, which proves how much he liked it. Good weather or foul. Me too.*

Mosquitoes don't like my blood. Once I was young enough to take offense at that, not understanding that rejection could be a blessing. So you can see why I liked walking the shore route home however muggy the weather. The sky is empty now, erased, but back then the Milky Way was common as dirt. Its light made everything a glamorous black-and-white movie. No matter what your place in life or your state of mind, having a star-packed sky be part of your night made you feel rich. And then there was the sea. Fishermen say there is life down there that looks like wedding veils and ropes of gold with ruby eyes. They say some sea life makes you think of the collars of schoolteachers or parasols made of flowers. That's what I was thinking about one hot night after a postponed birthday celebration. Off and on, whenever I felt like it, I stayed in my mother's house in Up Beach. I was on my way there that night, tired as a dog, when I saw Mr. Cosey with his shoes in his hand walking north back toward the hotel. I was up at the grass line, hoping to catch a breeze strong enough to get the smoke and sugar smell out of my uniform. He was further down, sloshing through the waves. I raised my hand and started to call out to him, but something—the way he held his head, maybe, or a kind of privacy wrapped about him—stopped me. I wanted to warn him but, weary and still out of sorts, I kept on walking. Down a piece I saw somebody else. A woman sitting on a blanket massaging her head with both hands. I stood there while she got up, naked as truth, and went into the waves. The tide was out, so she had to walk a long time for the water to reach her waist. Tall, raggedy clouds drifted across the moon and I remember how my heart kicked. Police-heads were on the move then. They had already drowned the Johnson boys, almost killed the cannery girl, and who knew what else they had in mind. But this woman kept on wading out into black water and I could tell she wasn't afraid of them—or of anything—because she stretched, raised her arms, and dove. I remember that arc better than I remember yesterday. She was out of sight for a time and I held my breath as long as she did. Finally, she surfaced and I breathed again watching her swim back to shallow water. She stood up and massaged her head once more. Her hair, flat when she went in, rose up slowly and took on the shape of the clouds dragging the moon. Then she— well, made a sound. I don't know to this day whether it was a word, a tune, or a scream. All I know is that it was a sound I wanted to answer. Even though, normally, I'm stone quiet, Celestial.

I don't deny her unstoppable good looks—they did arrest the mind—and while how she made her living saddened me, she did it in such a quiet, reserved way you would have thought she was a Red Cross nurse. She came from a whole family of sporting women although, unlike them, she had not understood the fatal attraction of gold teeth. Hers were white as snow. When Mr. Cosey changed—well, limited—her caseload, neither could break the spell. And the grave didn't change a thing.

I can watch my man from the porch. In the evening mostly, but sunrise too, when I need to see his shoulders collared with seafoam. There used to be white wicker chairs out here where pretty women drank iced tea with a drop of Jack Daniel's or Cutty Sark in it. Nothing left now, so I sit on the steps or lean my elbows on the railings. If I'm real still and listening carefully I can hear his voice. You'd think with all that strength, he'd be a bass. But, no. My man is a tenor.

5

LOVER

Sandler admitted he could have imagined the look but not the glisten. That was definite. Vida credited neither. The proof, she felt, was in her grandson's walk. Whatever the sign, both agreed that Romen was seeing someone, maybe even going with someone. They liked those terms—"seeing," "going with"—suggesting merely looking, accompanying. Not the furious coupling that produced the unmistakable look Sandler believed he had detected and a moist radiance he recognized at once. But Vida was right about the walk. Romen had developed a kind of strut to replace his former skulk. Of Sandler's feelings—resignation, pride, alarm, envy—he chose to focus on the last, trying to summon the memory of adolescent heat, its shield of well-being created by the accomplishment of being spent. He remembered his own maiden voyage (free of embarrassment, now) as a ferocity that had never mellowed into routine pleasure. Romen's entry might be as cherishable as it was enviable, and although it would probably end in foolishness or misery, it seemed unfair to cut off the boy's swagger when it was fresh. He believed toppling him now—introducing shame along with sound advice—was more likely to pervert future encounters without stopping them. So he watched the new moves, the attention to hygiene, the knowing smile replacing guffaws and sniggers, the condescension in his tone when he spoke to Vida. Most of all he savored the skin beauty as well as the ripple Vida noticed in his walk. Also, he appreciated the fact that Romen had stopped swinging his leg and grabbing his groin every minute in that obnoxious way that signaled more "want" than "have." Let him preen awhile, thought Sandler. Otherwise he might end up dog-chasing women his whole life. Forever on the prowl for a repeat of that first first time, he might end up like Bill Cosey had, wasting hours between the elbows of women whose names he couldn't remember and whose eyes he avoided. Except for one. Other

than her, Cosey had said, he never felt connected to a woman. His adored first wife
thought his interests tiresome, his appetite
abusive. So he chose the view he saw in the
eyes of local women, vacationers, slightly tipsy
vocalists whose boyfriends had not joined
them on the tour. Thus buoyed up and sim-
mered down, he had released his wife from
class, given her the hall pass she wanted. Or, in
Cosey's own words, "when kittens sleep, lions
creep."

"You wrong," Sandler replied. "Lions mate
for life."

"So do I," said Cosey, laughing softly. "So
do I."

Maybe, thought Sandler, but it was a mating
that had not changed Cosey's bachelor behavior, which, after years of eligible widower-
hood, he hoped to end by marrying a girl he
could educate to his taste. And if that had
worked out for him as planned, Cosey might
have limited his boat activity to fish caught
with a hook instead of a wallet. Sandler had
come to enjoy the fishing trips. Still in his
twenties, he didn't like to pal around with old
men, but since his father had moved away . . .
of course it wasn't like being with his own
father, but the conversation between them got
easier. Dipping a ball of cotton in bacon fat,

Sandler had smiled, saying, "My father taught me this."

Cosey looked at the bait. "You and him close?"

"Close enough."

"He still living?"

"Oh, yeah. Up north with my sister after Mama died. Old men feel better with their daughters. Young girls easier to push around." He caught himself and tried to clean it up in case Cosey was offended. "I wanted him to stay with us. I mean it's his house we living in. He's way too stubborn, but he must have his reasons."

"Fathers can be hard," answered Cosey, unaffected, it seemed, by the old man–young girl comment.

"Yours wasn't. I hear tell he left you a trunkful of money. That so?"

"Well, he had to leave it to somebody."

"My old man did all right by me too," said Sandler. "Not with money. Never had none, but I could always count on him, and he knows he can count on me no matter what."

"I hated mine."

"Sure enough?" Sandler was more surprised by the candor than the fact.

"Sure enough. He died on Christmas Day. His funeral was like a gift to the world."

That's the way their talk was when it was just the two of them. The one time Sandler was invited to one of Cosey's famous boat parties, he promised himself afterwards that he would never go again. Not just because of the company, although he was uncomfortable being jovial with middle-aged white men, one of whom was holstered; the well-to-do black men also made him feel out of place. The laughter was easy enough. And the three or four women stimulating it were pleasant. It was the talk, its tone, its lie that he couldn't take. Talk as fuel to feed the main delusion: the counterfeit world invented on the boat; the real one set aside for a few hours so women could dominate, men would crawl, blacks could insult whites. Until they docked. Then the sheriff could put his badge back on and call the colored physician a boy. Then the women took their shoes off because they had to walk home alone. One woman at the party stayed aloof, sober, slightly chiding. Deftly warding off advances, she never raised stakes or temperature. When Sandler asked him about her, Cosey said, "You can live with anything if you have what you can't live without." Clearly she was it, and in the photograph from which his portrait was painted, Sandler knew Cosey was looking at her. Hanging once in back of

Vida's desk, then above Heed Cosey's bed, the
face had a look he would recognize anywhere.
One that Romen was acquiring: first owner-
ship. Sandler knew that sometimes the first was
also the last and God help the boy if he got
soul-chained to a woman he couldn't trust.

But that was his male take on it. Vida would
certainly read it differently. The big question
now was, who. Who was the girl who bur-
nished skin and oiled a boy's stride? Romen
went to no parties, was home when told to be,
entertained no friends at home. Maybe she was
older, a grown woman with afternoon time on
her hands. But Romen's weekends and after-
school evenings were filled with chores. When
did he have time? Sandler put the question
to Vida, who was urging him to speak to
Romen.

"I need to know who it is before I start lec-
turing him," he said.

"What difference does it make?"

"I take it you content with his sheets?"

"I'll worry about the laundry," said Vida.
"You worry about VD. Which, by the way,
doesn't come with a biography. I work in a
hospital, remember? You have no idea what I
see."

"Well, I'm going to find out who she is."

"How?"

"I'll ask him."

"Sandler, he's not going to tell you."

"Must be a way. This is a wee little town and I don't want to wait until somebody's daddy or brother bangs on my door."

"People don't do that anymore. That was in our day. Did you bang on Plaquemain's door when he was courting Dolly?"

"Would have—if you hadn't been sold on him soon as he walked in the door."

"Be serious. Plaquemain had two years of college. Nobody around here could hold a candle to him."

"Thanks for reminding me. Now I think about it, maybe we should leave it up to his college-y father. When are they due?"

"Christmas, Dolly said."

"See there? Just three weeks."

"The girl could be pregnant by then!"

"Thought VD was worrying you."

"Everything is worrying me!"

"Come on, Vida. The boy doesn't stay out late; he cut loose those raggedy friends and you don't have to drag him out of bed anymore to go to school. He's ready before you are, and works good and steady at the Coseys'. Overtime, too."

"Oh, Lord," said Vida. "Oh my Lord."

"What?" Sandler looked at his wife and

then burst out laughing. "You have lost your natural mind, woman."

"Uh-uh," she said. "No I haven't. And 'steady' is the word, all right."

Suddenly Sandler saw thighs rising from tall black boots, and wondered again how icy the skin would be to the touch. And how smooth.

The boots, probably, which she never took off, freaked Romen as much as her nakedness—in fact, they made her more naked than if she had removed them. So it seemed natural to steal his grandfather's security uniform cap. It was gray, not black to match the boots, but it had a shiny visor, and when she put it on and stood there in just the cap and the boots, Romen knew his impulse was right. All of his impulses were right, now. He was fourteen doing an eighteen- or maybe twenty-year-old woman. Not only did she want him; she demanded him. Her craving was equal to his and his was bottomless. He could barely remember himself before November 12. Who was that wuss crying under a pillow because of some jive turkeys? Romen had no time for that sniveling self now. The halls of Bethune High were parade grounds; the congregation at the lockers was the audience of a prince. No more sidle along the walls or safety searches in crowds. And no trumpet blast to be heard. It was that simple.

When he approached the lockers that first day, they knew. And those who didn't, he told—in a way. Anybody who needed to get drunk, or tie somebody up, or required the company of a herd, was a punk. Two days earlier Theo would have knocked him into the wall. But on November 13, Romen had new eyes, ones that appraised and dared. The boys hazarded a few lame teases, but Romen's smile, slow and informed, kept them off balance. The clincher came from the girls. Sensing something capable in his manner, they stopped rolling their eyes and smothering giggles. Now they arched their backs, threw back their shoulders in great, long deceptive yawns. Now they cut question-and-answer glances his way. Not only had Romen scored, the score was big time. A teacher? they wondered. Somebody's older sister? He wouldn't say—even resisting the "Your mama" that rose to his lips. In any case, he had neck now. And when he wasn't stretching it, he was gazing through the classroom window dreaming of what had already taken place and imagining new ways to do it. The boots. The black socks. With the security cap she would look like an officer.

Hard enough to drill for oil, Romen adjusted his chair and tried to focus on the Eighteenth Amendment the teacher was explaining with such intensity he almost understood her. How was he supposed to concentrate on a history lesson when Junior's face was a study? Her breasts, her armpits required focused exploration; her skin demanded closer analysis. Was its perfume flowery or more like rain? Besides, he had to memorize the thirty-eight ways she could smile and what each one meant. He needed a whole semester to figure out her sci-fi eyes: the lids, the lashes, irises so shiny black she could be an alien. One he would kill to join on the spaceship.

Junior had use of the Coseys' car. To shop, go to the bank, post office, do errands Mrs. Cosey needed done and Miss Christine didn't want to do. So if he skipped sixth period, or if study hall preceded lunch, Junior picked him up on Prince Arthur Street and they drove to one of their preplanned spots. The plan (hers) was to make it everywhere. To map the county with grapple and heat. On the list, but not managed yet, was Bethune High (preferably in a classroom); the cineplex, the beach, the abandoned cannery, and the hotel. The phone booth on Baron Street near Softee's was her favorite, and so far they had accomplished only one other outside-her-bedroom adventure—a backseat adventure one evening in Café Ria's parking lot. Today he would meet her behind Videoland, for some fast stroking before she drove him to Monarch Street, where he would pull leaves from the gutters. Then she would drive him home, stopping maybe at a different phone booth on the way. Exciting as all that travel was to anticipate, indelible as this town was becoming (he sort of owned Café Ria now, and Theo too), nothing beat the sight of a straddling Junior in bed, booted, hatted, with a visor throwing her eyes into shadow. Theo, Jamal, and Freddie could keep whatever tenth-grade party girl in plastic heels they found. Where was the neck in that? No arms tightening but their own; no eager mouths but their own; no eeeee's of pleasure but their own. Most of all no privacy. Instead they needed a chorus of each other to back them up, make it real, help them turn down the trumpet screech in their own ears. All the time doing it, not to the girl but for, maybe even to, one another. He, on the other hand, gripped and nibbled on, had a woman of his own, one who stepped up and snatched privacy right in the middle of a stupid-blind public.

Romen raised his eyes to the clock. Two minutes—forever—before the bell.

LOVE

• • •

Junior kept the motor running. She had no driver's license and wanted to be in position to take off if noticed by a cop cruiser. She was hungry again. Two hours earlier she had eaten four strips of bacon, toast, and two eggs. Now she thought of getting burgers and shakes at Softee's to take back to Videoland. She could do two things at the same time. Even three. Romen would like that and so would her Good Man. Sometimes he sat at the foot of her bed—happy to watch her sleep, and when she woke he winked before he smiled and stepped away. Funny how being seen all the time, watched day and night at Correctional, had infuriated her, but being looked at by her Good Man delighted her. She didn't have to turn her head to know his foot was on the door saddle or that his fingers were drumming a windowsill. The aftershave announced his entrance. And if she was still enough, he might whisper: "Nice hair," "Take it," "Good girl," "Sweet tits," "Why not?" More understanding than any G.I. Joe. Her luck was still holding: a cushy, warm place to stay, a lot of really good food, a (paying) job—more than she expected when, because of her age, Correctional had to release her. But the bonus of Romen was like the plus sign after an A. The ones she got when she had been a model student. Considered model until they made it seem as though she had killed him. Why would she do that? Mess up just when she was about to graduate.

Killing the Administrator was not on her mind—stopping him was. Some girls liked his Conferences; traded them for Office Duty, sexy underwear, trips off campus. But not her. Junior, already prized for her keyboard skills, always had office work. Besides, cotton under-wear was just fine; and the thrill of off-campus trips was erased by the watchful eyes of towns-people as you strolled through the aisles, or put your elbows on the Burger King counter. Any-way, she got her sex from Campus A or from a girl crying for home. Who wanted or needed an old man (he must be thirty, at least) wearing a wide red tie pointing down to a penis that couldn't compete with raw vegetables, bars of soap, kitchen utensils, lollipops, or anything else inventive girls could conjure?

The Exit Conference was scheduled for Friday, and when he changed it to Monday, four days earlier, Junior thought a prize or a job offer would be discussed. At fifteen she was free to leave, purged of the wickedness that had landed her there, and return to her family, not one of whom had visited in the whole three years. She had no intention of going back to the Settlement. Correctional had saved her from them. But she did want to see the out-side-the-Settlement world; the televised one, the one new Correctional students talked about. Eagerness to get out would have pre-vented any last-minute infraction; her known good behavior would have disallowed it. Still, the Committee refused to believe her, believed the Administrator instead, and the Guidance Counselor who knew better.

The Exit Conference started out great. The Administrator, relaxed and talkative, described his hopes for Correctional, for her. He strolled to the sliding doors that opened onto a small balcony, invited her to join him and admire the grand trees surrounding. Perched on the railing, he suggested she do the same, congrat-ulating her, reminding her to keep in touch. He was there for her. Smiling, he told her she might want to get a haircut before she left. "Such beautiful hair, wild." He touched it, patting her head fondly, at first and then, drawing closer, pressed it. Hard. Junior dropped to her knees, and while the Adminis-trator's hands were busy unbelting, hers went to the back of his knees, upending him over the railing. He fell one story. Only one. The Guidance Counselor who saw him fall and rushed to his aid saw also the loosened belt and open fly. His testimony, arranged of course to keep his job, supported the Administrator, who was as confounded and bewildered as anybody at the "sudden, strange, self-loathing behavior" of a once model student. The Committee, pained by Junior's use of the word "lick" in her defense, quickly transferred her from student to inmate for a violence they could only shake their heads at.

Junior learned a lot in the next three years. If she ever had a moment's thought that after Correctional she would fail in life, the thought quickly evaporated. Reform, then Prison, refined her insight. In Correctional real time is not spent; it is deposited, bit by manageable bit. What to do for the next half hour, ten minutes. It will take seven minutes to do your nails; twenty to wash your hair. A minute and a half to get from gym to class. Games, ninety minutes. Two hours of television before lights-out and the falling-down years of sleeping while awake to the "there" of other people's bodies. Unlike what people thought, in the daily grid of activities, to plan was fatal. Stay ready, on tippy-toe. And read fast: gestures, eyes, mouths, tones of speech, body movement—minds. Gauge the moment. Recognize a chance. It's all you. And if you luck out, find yourself near an open wallet, window, or door, GO! It's all you. All of it. Good luck you found, but good fortune you made. And her Good Man agreed. As she knew from the beginning, he liked to see her win.

They recognized each other the very first night when he gazed at her from his portrait. But it was in dream they got acquainted. No fuss, no bother, no recriminations—he lifted her up to his shoulders, where she rode through an orchard of green Granny apples. When she woke in a bright, cold room, the dream-warmth was better than the blanket. A tub bath (at last) before eagerly climbing the stairs partly to show her new boss lady how punctual she was; mostly to catch another glimpse of her Good Man's shoulders. Heed was sitting in bed, the crown of her head just under the frame's gilt. Junior told her she didn't want to go pick up her clothes—that she would wear what she had on until she could afford new things. Heed directed her to a closet where a red suit hung in plastic. It was ugly and too big, but Junior was thinking how much she wanted to undress right there in Heed's bedroom while he watched.

"Get some breakfast and come right on back," said Heed.

She did: grapefruit, scrambled eggs, bacon,

grits—chatting with Christine in an old woman's suit.

It was when she had finished, on her way back to Heed, that she knew for sure. In the hallway on the second floor she was flooded by his company: a tinkle of glee, a promise of more; then her attention drawn to a door opposite the room she had slept in. Ajar. A light pomade or aftershave in the air. She stepped through. Inside, a kind of office with sofa, desk, leather chairs, dresser. Junior examined it all. She stroked ties and shirts in the closet; smelled his shoes; rubbed her cheek on the sleeve of his seersucker jacket. Then, finding a stack of undershorts, she took off the red suit, stepped into the shorts, and lay on the sofa. His happiness was unmistakable. So was his relief at having her there, handling his things and enjoying herself in front of him.

Later, on her way back to Heed's room, Junior looked over her shoulder toward the door—still ajar—and saw the cuff of a white shirtsleeve, his hand closing the door. Junior laughed, knowing as she did that he did too.

And wouldn't you know it? Right outside Heed's window was a boy. For her. Everything was becoming clear. If she pleased both women, they could live happily together. All she had to do was study them, learn them.

Christine didn't care about money, liked feeding her, and encouraged her to take the car.
Heed worried about gasoline prices and the
value of dated milk cartons and day-old bread.
Junior saw both Christine's generosity and
Heed's stinginess as forms of dismissal. One
was "Take what you need and leave me alone."
The other was "I'm in control and you are
not." Neither woman was interested in her—
except as she simplified or complicated their
relationship with each other. Not quite a go-
between, not quite a confidante, it was a
murky role in which she had discovered small
secrets. Among the new, never-worn clothes in
the locked suitcases were a short, sheer nightie,
aqua fuzz at the hem; a carton that explained
its contents as a douche bag; a jar of mustard-
yellow Massengill powder. Things needed
on vacation? For escape? Christine took a
bunch of vitamin pills and poured Michelob
into empty Pepsi cans. Both women regularly
bought and wore sanitary napkins, and threw
them in the trash completely unstained. Heed's
signature on a check was a press of her initials,
HC, rickety and slanting to the left.

In time the women would tire of their
fight, leave things to her. She could make it
happen, arrange harmony when she felt like it,
the way she had at Correctional when Betty

cut in on Sarah at the Christmas Dance and they had fought themselves into Isolation. Junior had brokered the peace when the girls returned, bristling, to the Common Room, threatening behavior that could ruin it for the whole of Mary House. Siding with each antagonist, she had become indispensable to both. How much harder could it be with women too tired to shop, too weak to dye their own hair? Too old to remember the real purpose of an automobile. He chuckled.

She gunned the motor. Vanilla? Strawberry? Romen was in view.

6

HUSBAND

Correctional girls knew better than to trust a label. "Let set for five minutes, then rinse thoroughly" was a suggestion, not an order. Some products needed fifteen minutes; others would cook the scalp instantly. Correctionals knew all about grooming: hair-braiding, curling, shampooing, straightening, cutting. And before coloring privileges were taken away—Fawn practically blinded Helen with a deliberate blast of Natural Instinct—they practiced tint-and-dye with professional single-mindedness.

Junior slid the tail of a fine-tooth comb through Heed's hair, then filled each silver valley with a thick stream of Velvet Tress. She had lubricated each parting with Vaseline to take down the pain of its lye. Then she tipped

Heed's head gently—this way and that—to check the nape and hairline. The rims of Heed's ears were lightly scarred, either from old dye burns or awkwardly held straightening combs. Junior ran a gloved forefinger slowly over the wounds. Then she bent the ear to blot the excess liquid with cotton. Satisfied that the roots were wet and steeping, she tucked the hair into a shower cap. Washing utensils, folding towels, she listened to Heed's drone—the voluptuous murmur that always accompanies hairdressing. Massage, caress by devoted hands, are natural companions to a warm-water rinse, to the shy squeak of clean hair. In a drowsy voice full of amusement Heed explained the barber's chair she was sitting in. How Papa said no chair in the world was more comfortable; that he had paid thirty dollars for it but it was worth hundreds. How home-decorating issues could not keep him from moving it from the hotel into the bathroom of their new house. How much Heed treasured it, because in the early days of their marriage it was in that very chair that he took pains to teach her how to manicure, pedicure, keep all his nails in perfect shape. And how to shave him, too, with a straight razor and strop. She was so little she had to stand on a stool to reach. But he was nothing but patience, and she learned.

Encouraged by Junior's obedient but interested silence, she went on to say she never felt clean enough in those early days. Folks from her neighborhood were mocked for living near a fish factory, and although she had never worked one minute in the place, she suspected she was suspected of its blight. Even now it was the worst thing about her hands, how limited her habits of hygiene had become.

Junior wondered if Heed was trying to ask for a pedicure as well as a bathing hand. Although it was not the fun of group showers at Correctional, soaping a body—any body— held a satisfaction only a Settlement child could know. Besides, it pleased him to see her taking care of his wife; as it pleased him to watch her and Romen wrestle naked in the backseat of his twenty-five-year-old car; just as it tickled him to know she was wearing his shorts.

She turned on the blow dryer. Warm, then cool air played on Heed's scalp, stimulating more reminiscence.

"We were the first colored family in Silk and not a peep out of one white mouth. Nineteen forty-five. The war was just over. Everybody had money but Papa had more than most, so he built this house on land as far as you could see. It's Oceanside now, but then it was a run-down orchard full of birds. Hand me the towel."

Heed patted her temples and looked in the mirror.

"We had two victory celebrations. One at the hotel for the public; and a private one here at the house. People talked about it for years. That whole summer was a party; started in May and ended August 14. Flags everywhere. Firecrackers and rockets on the beach. Meat was rationed, but Papa had black-market connections so we had a truckload. I wasn't allowed in the kitchen, but they needed me then."

"Why wouldn't they let you in the kitchen?"

Heed wrinkled her nose. "Oh, I wasn't much of a cook. Besides, I was the wife, you know; the hostess, and the hostess never . . ."

Heed stopped. Memory of "hostessing" those two kinds of victory parties in 1945 was swamped by another pair of celebrations, two years later. A sixteenth-birthday-plus-graduation party for Christine. Again, a family dinner at the house preceding a public celebration at the hotel. In June of 1947, Heed had not seen her used-to-be friend in four years. The Christine that stepped out of Papa's

Cadillac was nothing like the one who, in 1943, had left home rubbing tears from her cheeks with her palm. The eyes above those cheeks had widened—and cooled. Two braids had become a pageboy smooth as the wearer's smile. They did not pretend to like each other and, sitting at the table, hid curiosity like pros. The sun, dipping and red as watermelon, left its heat behind—moist and buzzing. Heed remembered the baby-powder smell from the bowl of gardenias, their edges browning like toast. And hands: a casual wave at a fly, a dinner napkin pressed to a damp upper lip; Papa's forefinger playing his mustache. In silence they waited for L. She had cooked a sumptuous meal and prepared a cake. Sixteen candles waited to be lit in a garden of sugar roses and ribbons of blue marzipan. The conversation had been polite, hollow, stressed by the grating ceiling fan and meaningful looks between May and Christine. Papa, in the grip of postwar excitement, had talked about his plans to improve the hotel, including a Carrier air-cooling system.

"Wouldn't that be wonderful," said Christine. "I had forgotten how hot it gets here."

"We'll do the hotel first," said Cosey. "Then the house."

Heed, feeling a flush of authority, chimed in. "The bedroom fans is in good shape, but I do feel badly about the one in this room."

"You mean 'bad.' You feel 'bad.' "

"That's what I said."

"You said 'badly.' 'Feel' is an intransitive verb in your sentence and is modified by an adjective. If you really mean you feel 'badly,' then you are saying something like 'My fingers are numb and therefore they don't touch things well.' Now if you—"

"Don't you sit at my table and tell me how to talk."

"Your table?"

"Be quiet, you two. Please? Just be quiet."

"Whose side you on?"

"Do what I say, Heed."

"You taking her side!" Heed stood up.

"Sit down, you hear me?"

Heed sat down in the thumping silence, aware of magnified hands and gardenia petals until L entered with a champagne bucket. In her presence Heed calmed enough to hold up her glass for the pouring.

"The other one," he said. "That's a water glass."

May didn't try to hide her glee as she exchanged glances with her daughter. When Heed caught the smile, the look, she burst out of herself and, throwing the incorrect glass at her husband, rushed past him toward the stairs. Papa rose and grabbed her arm. Then with a kind of old-timey grace, he put her across his knee and spanked her. Not hard. Not cruel. Methodically, reluctantly, the way you would any other brat. When he stopped there was no way for her to get out of the room onto the stairs. No way at all, but she made it. The conversation that picked up as she stumbled up the stairs was relaxed, as though an awful smell that had been distracting the guests had been eliminated at last.

Junior cut off the dryer. "What about your own family? You never talk about them."

Heed made a sound in her throat and waved a fin.

Junior laughed. "I know what you mean. I'd swallow lye before I'd live with my folks. They made me sleep on the floor."

"That's funny," said Heed. "First few weeks after my wedding, I couldn't sleep anywhere but. That's how used to it I was."

Heed glanced at Junior's face in the mirror, thinking: That's what it is, what made me take her on. We're both out here, alone. With fire ants for family. Marriage was a chance for me to get out, to learn how to sleep in a real bed, to have somebody ask you what you wanted to eat, then labor over the dish. All in a big hotel where clothes were ironed and folded or hung on hangers—not nails. Where you could see city women sway on a dance floor; hide behind the stage to watch musicians tune up and singers fix their underwear or take a final sip before going on to sing "In the dark, in the dark . . ." Right after the wedding, her own family had begun to swarm and bite for blood. Whatever it cost in humiliation, the Coseys were (had become) her family. Although it turned out she had to fight for her place in it, Papa made it possible. When he was around everybody backed off. Time after time he made it clear—they would respect her. Like the time they came back from their three-day "honeymoon." Heed was bursting with stories to tell Christine. Wobbling in her new sling-back pumps, half falling up the steps, she was met not just by May's scorn but Christine's sulk as well.

May, of course, started it, laughing aloud at Heed's new clothes; but Christine joined in with a smirk Heed had never seen before.

"What in God's name have you got on?" said May, holding her forehead. "You look like a, a . . ."

"Whoa. Whoa," said Papa. "I'm not having that. Both of you—quit it. You hear me?"

Trembling, Heed looked to Christine for help. There wasn't any. Her friend's eyes were cold, as though Heed had betrayed her, instead of the other way around. L came forward with a scissors and cut the price tag hanging from Heed's sleeve. What, she wondered, are they laughing at? The Cuban heel shoes? The black net stockings? The pretty purple suit? Papa had been charmed with her purchases. He had taken her to a fine department store that did not have a "No Colored" sign or policy, where you could use the bathroom, try on hats (they put tissue inside the crown), and undress in a special room in the back. Heed picked out things glamorous women in the hotel wore and believed that the wide smile of the clerk and the merry laughter of other customers showed their delighted approval of her choices. "You look like a dream," one of them said, and sputtered with pleasure. As she came out of the dressing room in a creamy beige dress with red silk roses sewed at the shoulder, the low-cut bosom gathered for breasts some-where in her future, Papa smiled, nodded, and said, "We'll take it. We'll take it all."

Every day for three days they shopped, Papa letting her buy anything she wanted, including Parisian Night lipstick. They played "wrestle" in the morning, then ate lunch at Reynaud's.

Unlike their hotel, the one they stayed in had
no dining room, which pleased Papa, who was
always looking for colored businesses less satisfactory than his. He took her to Broad Street,
Edwards Bros., Woolworth's, Hansons, where
she bought not just high-heeled shoes but
huaraches, shiny bedroom slippers, and fishnet
hose. Only in the evening was she alone, for a
few hours while he visited friends, tended
to business. None of which Heed minded,
because she had coloring books, picture magazines, paper dolls to cut out and clothe. Then
there was the street. From their second-floor
window, she watched in gaping fascination the
people and traffic below. Black square-topped
automobiles, bleating. Soldiers, sailors, women
in tiny hats like pincushions. Vegetable stands
in front of "Uncle Sam Wants You" posters.

Papa took her to see *How Green Was My Valley, Kitty Foyle.* She sobbed so loud and long
at *The Grapes of Wrath,* his handkerchief was
squeezing wet. Wonderful as the honeymoon
was, she could hardly wait to get back and tell
Christine all about it. Hurt by her reception,
she kept her stories to herself. The one time
she tried to make peace with Christine, offering to let her wear her wedding ring, the
kitchen exploded. The four of them—May, L,
Christine, and Heed—were preparing vegeta-

bles when Heed slipped off the ring, held it out to Christine, and said, "You can wear it, if you want."

"You little fool!" May shouted.

Even L turned on her. "Watch yourself," she said. "The streets don't go there."

Christine burst out crying and ran through the back door. From the rain barrel, Heed could hear her shouting: "Ou-yidagay a ave-slidagay! E-hidagay ought-bidagay ou-yidagay ith-widagay a ear's-yidagay ent-ridagay an-didagay a andy-cidagay ar-bidagay!"

Heed examined the string beans as closely as she could while "Ave-slidagay! Ave-slida-gay!" rang in her head.

That night when Christine was dragged back by Chief Buddy Silk from a foolish attempt to run away, and got slapped in the face for it, Heed did not speak one word to her. Instead, she stood on the stairs with Papa and took his hand in hers. Two weeks later, Christine was gone, leaving Heed fending for herself. L and Papa her saviors in that puzzling world.

"I never knew my daddy," said Junior. "He was killed in the army. Vietnam."

"At least he went," said Heed.

"And my mother didn't care a thing about me."

"Mine, neither."

"Maybe I should get married, like you did."

"Be careful."

"Well, you got this nice big house out of it."

"My Vietnam. Except I come out alive." So far, she thought. "But like you say, he did leave me well off."

"See there? Aren't you glad he felt sorry for you?"

"Sorry?" Heed bristled. "What makes you say that?"

"Well, not 'sorry.' I didn't mean that. I meant he must have known you'd be all alone."

"Of course he did. But that wasn't pity. It was, it was . . ." She couldn't say it, and after 1947, she never heard him say it either. Not to her, anyway, and she listened for twenty-four years. The screams that shot from her mouth when he died were in recognition that she would never hear the word again.

"Listen." She reached back to touch Junior's elbow. "There is something I want you to do for me. Together. We have to do it together. There's something in it for you as well as me."

"Sure. What?"

"There's some documents I need. But they're in a place I can't get to by myself.

You'll have to take me there and then you have to help me find them."

"Take you where?"

"To the hotel. The attic. We'll need a fountain pen."

Junior couldn't find him. She looked for him in the other rooms, because when she was sitting in his study and wearing his tie, there was no trace of aftershave; no "Hey, sweet thing" whispered in her ear. Maybe she didn't need him to tell her. To approve. Maybe he took for granted she'd know what to do. First, check on Christine; make sure they were still friendly in case Heed's plans went bust. Getting Heed out to the car unseen by Christine should be easy, since the house schedule was as reliable as Correctional's.

That evening, she squatted near Christine, who was sitting on the back porch with a soda can in one hand and a cigarette in the other. Indifferent to the chilly weather, Christine wore a sleeveless blouse under her apron. Junior pointed to the cigarette pack.

"Can I have one?"

"Buy your own. You get paid. I don't."

"Suppose I can't afford it, Christine."

"You can afford that metal in your nose, you can afford cigarettes."

"Well, I don't smoke anyway. Stinks."

Christine laughed, thinking of the waft Junior had brought into the house the day she came. "Good for you," she said.

"How come you don't get paid? You work harder than me."

"Because your boss lady is insane as well as evil and needs help."

"I help her."

"Not that kind of help. You don't notice anything strange about her?"

"A little. Maybe."

"A little? Who don't leave a room for years but a demented person? What you all talk about up there, anyway?"

"Stuff. Her life."

"Oh, God."

"She showed me pictures. Wedding pictures. I saw a beautiful picture of you at her wedding. You were hot, Christine, really hot. You've known her a long time, right? You cousins or something?"

"Cousins?" Christine's lips curled.

"You're not related? Just friends?"

"She is not my friend. She's my grand-mother."

"Say what?"

"You heard me. Grandmother. Get it?"

"But you're the same age."

"I'm older. Eight months older."

"Wait a minute." Junior frowned. "She said she was married for thirty years and he died twenty-five years ago. So she must have been . . . a baby."

"Mention was made." Christine sipped from the can.

"And you were . . . how old?"

"Twelve. My grandfather married her when she was eleven. We were best friends. One day we built castles on the beach; next day he sat her in his lap. One day we were playing house under a quilt; next day she slept in his bed. One day we played jacks; the next she was fucking my grandfather." Christine surveyed her diamonds, waved her fingers like a hula dancer. "One day this house was mine; next day she owned it."

She put her cigarettes away and stood up. "It does something to the mind, marrying before your first period. She needs professional help, don't you think?" Christine blew on her rings. "There's virgins and then there's children," she said, and left Junior to ponder the thought.

Back in the kitchen, Christine began to perspire. She put her forehead against the refrigerator door, then opened it for the cool air. The wave of heat receded, as it had outside on the steps, but returned quickly and left her trembling. It had been a while since the veil parted to expose a wide plateau of lifeless stone and she wondered if it was she, not Heed, who needed professional care. Extracting some ice cubes, she wrapped them in a towel, touching her throat, temples, wrists until she felt steady. The bleakness remained. A clear sight of the world as it was—barren dark ugly without remorse. What was she doing here? Her mind scurried; her motives pointless. She knew she was playing busy, but how else to set it aside—the bleak rock stripped of green? Closing her eyes, the cold towel pressed against her lids, she whispered No! and straightened her spine. This *was* important. Her struggle with Heed was neither mindless nor wasted. She would never forget how she had fought for her, defied her mother to protect her, to give her clothes: dresses, shorts, a bathing suit, sandals; to picnic alone on the beach. They shared stomachache laughter, a secret language, and knew as they slept together that one's dreaming was the same as the other one's. Then to have your best and only friend leave the squealing splash in your bathtub, trade the stories made up and whispered beneath sheets in your bed for a dark room at the end of the hall reeking of liquor and an old man's business, doing things no one would describe but were so terrible no one could ignore them. She would not forget that. Why should she? It changed her life. It changed May *for* life. Even L's jaw dropped.

After the wedding, they tried to play together occasionally, but with each one lying in wait for the other's insult, the efforts ended in quarrel. Then tears, May's hand gripping; words hissed lest Grandpa Cosey hear you mocking his bride.

There was a heap of blame to spread. He was the Big Man who, with no one to stop him, could get away with it and anything else he wanted. Then there was her mother, who chose to send her away rather than confront him. Put her in a faraway school and discouraged summer vacations at home. For her own good, she said, arranging church camps and summers with classmates. Once May enrolled her as a counselor in a settlement house for Negro girls who had run away rather than be mistreated at home. Never mind Christmas packages in the mail, expensive, wrong-size shoes in September; in spite of envelopes fat with lies and money, the rejection was obvious. L, too, was to blame; she was the only peacemaker around, whether glaring or shak-

ing her head, but she would take no one's side.
The real betrayal, however, lay at the feet of the
friend who grinned happily as she was led
down the hall to darkness, liquor smell, and
old-man business. So who had to go? Who had
to leave her bedroom, her playhouse, the sea?
The only innocent one in the place, that's
who. Even when she returned, a sixteen-year-
old, poised and ready to take her place in the
family, they threw her away, because by then
Heed had become grown-up-nasty. Mean
enough to set her on fire.

Christine went to her room and sat down in
the worn recliner she preferred to the scratchy
sofa. The perspiration was ebbing; the dizziness
receding. The melancholy persisted. I must
have been the one who dreamed up this
world, she thought. No nice person could
have.

It should have been different. She meant it
to be different. On the train, heading home
from Maple Valley, she had carefully planned
her attitude, her behavior. Everything would
come off nicely, since her return began with a
celebration celebrating everything: her birthday, graduation, the new house. She was deter-
mined to be civil to Heed, in control, but
nicely so, the way they were taught to behave
at Maple Valley. How or why she got lured into

showing off about grammar, she couldn't recall. What she most remembered was her grandfather spanking Heed, and the flood of pleasure that came when he took his grand-daughter's side against his wife's, for a change, taking steps to show the kind of behavior he prized. Christine's delight was deep and rampant as the three of them—the real Coseys—left together, drove off in the big automobile, the unworthy one nowhere to be seen.

When she and May returned, smoke was billowing from her bedroom window. Racing screaming into the house and up the stairs, they found L smothering the blackened sheets with a twenty-pound sack of sugar, carameliz-ing evil.

Again, it was Christine, not Heed, who had to leave. Grandfather Cosey had left the hotel party abruptly to go nobody knew where. Afraid and angry, mother and daughter stayed awake seething until 3 a.m., when he came back, barefoot as a yard dog, holding his shoes in his hand. Instead of locating Heed to throw her back where she came from, he laughed.

"She's going to kill us," May hissed.

"The bed was empty," he said, still chuck-ling.

"Tonight it was! What about tomorrow?"

"I'll speak to her."

"Speak? Speak? Bill, please!" May was begging.

"Calm down, May. I said I'd take care of it." He moved as though the conversation was over and he needed rest. May touched his elbow.

"What about Christine? She can't live here like this. It's dangerous."

"It won't happen again," he said, hitting the word "won't."

"She's dangerous, Bill. You know she is."

He looked at May then, for what seemed an age, and nodded. "You may be right." Then, touching his mustache, "Is there somewhere she can go for a week or two?"

"Heed?"

"No," he said, surprised at the suggestion, then frowning. "Christine."

"But Heed started the fire. She's the guilty one. Why should Christine leave?"

"I'm not married to Christine. I married Heed. Besides, it will only be for a little while. Till things get settled around here."

Just like that, Christine is to be packed off, sent away to the house of a classmate. For a week or two. A "vacation," they will tell people, whether anyone believed it or not. Christine will call and May will get on the line, make arrangements.

Standing there in a movie star's gown, rhinestones glittering its top, Christine made up her own mind. He never once looked at her. He had laughed. His cheap little bitch-wife had tried to kill her—sort of—and might succeed one day would he laugh then too would he look finally at the charred flesh of his own flesh and settle that also as though it were a guest's bounced check or a no-show musician or a quarrel with a salesman who had shortchanged an order of Scotch whiskey? Later, for a visit with a classmate. Later, crazies. Put on your shoes, old man, and look at me good now, because you will never see me again.

You are always thinking about death, I told her. No, she said. Death is always thinking about me. She didn't know squat about it. She thought death was going to heaven or hell. It never occurred to her it might be just more of the same. You could do anything you wanted except you're doing it all by yourself. But that was May's way of explaining why she hoarded and buried, and preserved and stole. Death was trying to pry open the door, and she needed all her cunning to stave him off. Her daughter was the loose hinge, a weakness that could lead to the loss of everything. Christine had to be defended not only from what had come in and snatched her father but from the live death of poverty, the Negro kind May was familiar with. Unhoused, begging; their Christian faith demanding never-ending gratitude for a plate of hominy. Other than disapproving white folk, nothing scared her more. She gave herself every opportunity to recount how Mr. Cosey came from a long line of quiet, prosperous slaves and thrifty freedmen—each generation adding to the inheritance left by the previous one. Independent contractors, she called them. Cobblers, seamstresses, carpenters, ironmongers, blacksmiths, unpaid laborers, and craftsmen who refined their skills, narrowed and pointed them for rich folks who would gift and tip them. The carpenters made fine pianos; the ironmongers served a local college laboratory. One, a blacksmith, took his craft to a horse farm where he made himself first reliable, then indispensable, then profitable. In that position his claim to wages instead of shelter was accepted. Little by little, the story went, they gathered and held on to what they earned for offspring they told and taught to do better. But they kept low, no bragging, no sass—just curry and keep close relationships with the whites who mattered. That was the street-sweet story, anyway—the one that belonged to somebody else that she and Mr. Cosey took for themselves. He knew better, but May believed it and that's why little Heed with a man's undershirt for a dress looked to her like the end of all that—a bottlefly let in through the door, already buzzing at the food table and, if it settled on Christine, bound to smear her with the garbage it was born in. She had put up with the girls' friendship until Mr. Cosey messed with it. Then she had to figure something out fast. If Heed and Christine had ideas about being friends and behaving like sisters just because a reckless old reprobate had a whim, May put a stop to them. If she couldn't swat the bottlefly, she could tear its wings, Raid-spray the air so it couldn't breathe—or turn her daughter into an ally.

Pity. They were just little girls. In a year they would be bleeding—hard. Skin clear and death-defying. They had no business in that business.

The day Mr. Cosey told us who he was marrying was the opening day of May's personal December 7. In an eye blink she went from defense to war. And as any honest veteran can tell you, war is good for the lonely; an outright comfort to the daft. She wasn't always like that. When I first saw her in 1929 standing next to Billy Boy she looked just like what she was: the last daughter of an itinerant preacher who had to accept clothes from any congregation he could attract. A pretty, undercherished girl in an over-mended coat. The little scrap of fur collar, the lettuce-green dress and black-and-white pumps put you right away in mind of a rummage sale. And while I was wondering where Mr. Cosey's son found her, she raised Billy Boy's hand to her mouth and kissed it. The way her eyes ate everything, traveling up and around the hotel lobby, I thought she would behave like a guest expecting to be waited on. I was dead wrong about that. She put off unpacking her cardboard suitcase; just changed out of that hand-me-down dress and started in. "Let's," she said in a soft, sweet voice. "Let's polish this. Let's move that, clean under here, wipe there . . ." How could we help but smile? Her meringue voice, her ladylike manners. Mr. Cosey most of all, seeing his son had chosen a wife certain to be a plus.

She moved Billy Boy from waiting tables to tending bar and then booking performers, which left Mr. Cosey free to think about money and play. Even pregnancy didn't slow her down. May was the first mother I saw who weaned her baby at three months. When Billy Boy died in '35, he went so fast we didn't have time to tend him. Christine crawled under my bed, and when I found her there, I let her sleep with me. She was never a crying child, so listening to her whimpering in her sleep was a comfort to me, since May looked on Billy Boy's death as more of an insult than a tragedy. Dry-eyed as a turtle, she left Christine to me to raise. Mr. Cosey sank low so it was left to May and me to keep things up and going. For the next seven years she put all her *energy into the hotel's business. Seven years of her hard work were rewarded with "I'm taking a wife. You know her. Christine's little friend." Rewarded by watching her father-in-law marry her twelve-year-old daughter's playmate and put that playmate ahead of everything, including herself, her daughter, and all she had worked for. Not only that. She was supposed to teach and train the playmate to take charge of us. Most people married young back then (the sooner a girl was taken over by a man, the better), but eleven? It was worrisome for sure, but there was more to it than age. May's new mother-in-law was not just a child, she was a Johnson. In no wild dream could she have invented a family that scared her more. The fool on German Syrup labels. The savage on Czar's Baking Powder. The brain-dead on Alden's Fruit Vinegar, Korn Kinks Cereal, J. J. Coates Thread, and the flyblown babies on Sanford's Ginger. That's who she saw when she looked at the Johnsons. She might be braiding her hair in the bedroom, patting cool water on her temples in the kitchen, wherever she was her talk was the same: shiftlessness was not a habit, it was a trait; ignorance was destiny; dirt lingered on by choice. She shuddered when she said that, being the daughter of a preacher, she really tried to dredge up Christian charity, but failed whenever she looked at a Johnson. Or heard about them. Listen to their names, she said. Overblown names people give to mules and fishing boats. Bride. Welcome Morning. Princess Starlight. Righteous Spirit. Solitude. Heed the Night. Add to that the main calamity—the unapologetic shiftlessness of the parents, Wilbur and Surrey, who thought sitting in a rowboat with a string was work. Having lost two children to the seabed, they used their grief first like a begging cup, then as a tax levied on their neighbors. So why not let their youngest girl marry a fifty-two-year-old man for who knew how much money changed hands. If he gave them a two-dollar bill, May said, a dollar and fifty cents refund was due. But we all knew Mr. Cosey never bought anything cheap—or if he did, it came to have value in time. Like a child who would soon grow up and bear other children. Which brings me to the other thing bothering May. The Johnsons were not just poor and trifling, their girls were thought to be mighty quick in the skirt-raising department. So what must have attracted Mr. Cosey to Heed in the first place could infect her own daughter. Before May had even begun instruction about menstruation, or thought of sheltering Christine from unsuitable boys, her home was throbbing with girl flesh made sexy, an atmosphere that Christine might soak up faster than a fruitcake soaks up rum. And all because Mr. Cosey wanted children.*

Well, that's what he told his friends and maybe himself. But not me. He never told that to me because I had worked for him since I was fourteen and knew the truth. He liked her. Besides, like a lot of folk did when war plants desegregated, his sporting woman left town. That was the truth, but not all of it. I remember him telling me a tale about some child who fell down in horse manure running after a posse and how the white folks laughed. So cruel, the crowd enjoying themselves at murder. He repeated it every time he needed an example of heartless whites, so I supposed the point was he laughed too and apologized for it by marrying Heed. Just like he avoided Christine because she had his father's gray eyes, he picked Heed to make old Dark groan. I've come to believe every family has a Dark and needs one. All over the world, traitors help progress. It's like being exposed to tuberculosis. After it fills the cemetery, it strengthens whoever survives; helps them know the difference between a strong mind and a healthy one; between the righteous and the right—which is, after all, progress. The problem for those left alive is what to do about revenge—how to escape the sweetness of its rot. So you can see why families make the best enemies. They have time and convenience to honey-butter the wickedness they prefer. Shortsighted, though. What good does it do to keep a favorite hate going when the very person you've poisoned your life with is the one (maybe the only one) able or willing to carry you to the bathroom when you can't get there on your own? I sat at the foot of

May's bed or on top of her dresser sometimes and watched Heed soap her bottom, mash badly cooked food to just the right consistency. She cut May's toenails and wiped white flakes from her eyelids. The girl May lived to mistreat was the one she depended on to hold her head over the slop jar. Nagging her every second, but doing it: airing, cleaning, spooning, rubbing, turning her over to the cooler side of the bed on nights hot enough to make you cry. And there's not much sense in wasting time and life trying to put a woman in the asylum just to end up chipping ice for her to suck on. Where's the gain in setting fire to the nest you live in if you have to live in the ashes for fifty years? I saw what Mr. Cosey did to Heed at the birthday dinner. My heart reached out to her and I let him know it. While he fumbled for something in his pocket and May and Christine were waiting in the car, I tapped him on the shoulder. "Don't you never lay a hand on her again no matter what. Do, and I'm long gone." He looked at me with Billy Boy's eyes and said, "I made a mistake, L. A big mistake." "Tell her," I said. All I got was a sigh for an answer, and if I hadn't been so agitated I would have known right then who he was sighing over.

I never did learn what really happened at the dance, but my mother didn't knit me. Soon as they left I knew Heed was up to something. She tele-

phoned one of the hotel waiters; told him to come get her. About an hour or so after she left I heard a truck drive up and a door slam. Then high heels running across the hall. Not five minutes passed when I smelled smoke. I had the sense to climb up there with a pail of water and had to run back and forth from the bathroom sink to fill it, but water's no use with mattress fire. You think it's out, but deep in there it's waiting, biding its time till you turn your back. Then it eats the whole place up. I hauled the biggest sack of sugar I could find up there. When May and Christine got back the bed was quiet, like syrup.

Heed never admitted or denied the fire and I used to wonder why, if she was mad at him, she took it out on Christine instead. I don't wonder anymore. And I don't wonder why his mood stayed pleasant when he heard what Heed had done. May, naturally, was unforgiving and, twenty-eight years later, still loved the sight of her enemy forced to feed her. More satisfying than if her daughter had been her nurse— which she was eventually.

Heed snarled, as you would expect, at Christine's break-in, but she was happy to shift May onto her. And just in case Christine looked at the job, changed her mind, and left, Heed took to her bed and let her hands fold. At first I thought May would be relieved by her daughter's return, even though Christine was a big disappointment to her. Their quarrels were name-calling contests separated by years of nothing. So I was surprised at May's reaction. She was afraid. Not sure if her daughter could be trusted with a pillow. But Christine jumped right in with beautiful cooking and plants to fill the room, both of which, if truth be told, hurried the sick woman along. Christine played prodigal girl for a year or so, then, on one of the prettiest dawns, May died. Smiling.

I don't know what the smile was about. Nothing she aimed for had gone her way—except for the hatchet she threw between Heed and Christine when they were little girls. That stuck. Cleaved the ground they stood on. So when Christine leaned in to wipe crumbs from her mother's chin, May saw a familiar look in her daughter's eyes. Like before, they whispered about Heed, refreshed themselves with old stories of how she tried to trick them into believing she could write; the chop that fell to the floor because she couldn't manage the knife; how her coddling of Mr. Cosey failed to limit him to her sheets; the hat she chose for his funeral. Mother and daughter became friends at last. Decades of bitterness, sealed in quarrels over Malcolm X, Reverend King, Selma, Newark, Chicago, Detroit, and Watts were gone. Dead the question of what was best for the race, because Heed answered it for them. She was the throwback they both had fought. Neither won, but they agreed on the target, so I guess that's why May smiled into that lovely dawn.

Heed closed her fingers. Christine decorated hers. No matter. They battled on as though they were champions instead of sacrifices. A crying shame.

7

GUARDIAN

"I don't know what to say to the boy."

"Well, think of something. Fast. Or I will."

"What? What can you tell him?"

"The purpose of a zipper. The responsibility of a father. The mortality rate of AIDS."

"AIDS?"

"Who knows where she's been or with who? Who is she, anyway? Got no people, nobody ever heard of her. Dresses like a street woman. Acts like a, a . . ."

"She wouldn't be working for them if she wasn't all right. Had references or some such."

"You senile or just pretending?"

"Look who's talking."

"Christine has a reputation make Jezebel cringe, and Heed's a Johnson, remember."

"What's that supposed to mean?"

"It means morals of any kind whatsoever are not known in that family. What would Heed, who got married at the ripe old age of eleven, know about morals, restraint . . ."

"She never ran around on Cosey and you know she never condoned Christine's past. You can't blame her for what her daddy did."

"No, but I can take note of what her daddy is. Did she or didn't she try to burn her own house down?"

"I never did believe that."

"Well, the seed don't fall far from the pod. If they take in that kind of girl to work for them, what else might be going on over there? How can you trust either one of them? Just because Heed lets Romen clean her yard doesn't mean she's changed."

"Changed from what?"

"From a deceitful bitch who has to control people."

"I thought this was about Romen's behavior."

"It is. Behavior influenced by an ex-hooker and a witch. Listen, Sandler, I am not about to be a great-grandmother or an unpaid nurse or a deep pocketbook for some trashy teen mama just because you don't know what to say to a fourteen-year-old boy. Besides, we're responsible for Romen. Our own daughter expects us to be. Counts on us to be."

Sandler grunted and let his wife's argument, point by point, roll on. He did know what to say to Romen, but he knew it wouldn't matter. Forbidding it would just make the whole thing hotter, more enticing. He wouldn't be telling him to choose one girl over another, but to give up the only one he had complete physical access to. Like telling a duck not to waddle. He would have to think up something else. Condoms at the least, but Vida expected more—an end to the relationship. Add to that improbability the fact that he thought Romen was handling things pretty well, considering. He wasn't doping, ganged up, courting arrest, and his house manners had definitely improved. But Vida was right. The neighborhood had changed and so had the times. They didn't know the girl, had no recent knowledge of what the Cosey women might be up to. Just gossip, speculation, and grudges from local people who didn't know any more than they did. Once upon a time, everybody knew everything. Once upon a time, a man could speak to another about his son or daughter; or a group of women would swoop down on a fast girl. Except the Johnsons. Nobody swooped down on them. They were not typical, even in Up Beach, where people lived on top of one another and every cough, every sidelong look, was monitored.

Oh, Christ, he thought, that was fifty years ago. What was the point in remembering the good old days as though the past was pure? He knew for a fact it was simply stifled. Vida, in her tale of wickedness, had not said a word about Bill Cosey. She acted as though Heed had chased and seduced a fifty-two-year-old man, older than her father. That she had chosen to marry him rather than having been told to. Vida, like most people, probably resented the child because she stayed married to him, liked it, and took over his business. In their minds she was born a liar, a gold digger unable to wait for her twelfth birthday for pay dirt. They forgave Cosey. Everything. Even to the point of blaming a child for a grown man's interest in her. What was she supposed to do? Run away? Where? Was there someplace Cosey or Wilbur Johnson couldn't reach?

He had seen Heed more recently than anyone the day he knocked on the door and asked her if she could take Romen on as after-school help. She was civil. Neat as a pin, as always. Offered him iced coffee, probably to let him see Christine's status in the house. Sandler had always found her less of a pain than others had.

Because of his friendship with her husband, he guessed. Her edges were smoothed by his recollection of Bill Cosey telling him that he had not touched her until her period came; waited a year and only then took her on a honeymoon for the initiation. Still, she was not easy to be around. He couldn't say whether she was good-looking or not because "false," "touchy," were the words that came to his mind about her. False the way anybody would be who had jumped from a log to a castle overnight. Touchy the way anybody would be who had envy plus May on her back. But what Sandler saw was nothing like what Bill Cosey must have seen. For him it was as though twenty-five years hadn't happened. The Heed that Cosey reminisced about in his cups on the boat—as though she were dead—was not a frowning woman always on the lookout for a slight, a chance to find fault, but a long-legged angel with candle eyes and a smile he couldn't help but join.

Uneasy with other men's sexual confidences (he certainly wasn't providing any of his own), Sandler always made it his business to change the subject. But he remembered Cosey's dream-bitten expression as he rambled on about his first sight of Heed: hips narrow, chest smooth as a plank, skin soft and damp, like a lip. Invisible navel above scant, newborn hair. Cosey never explained the attraction any other way, except to say he wanted to raise her and couldn't wait to watch her grow. That the steady, up-close observation most men don't know the pleasure of kept him not just true but lively. Listening to Cosey's rapturous description of his wife, Sandler was not as repelled as he'd expected to be, since the picture that emerged from the telling called to his mind not a child but a fashion model. Although by then Cosey was fully involved with grown women, the memory of having a child bride still stirred him. Vida had nothing to say about that, and Sandler didn't want the misery of bringing it up, of tilting his wife's idol with a blow of insight.

Oh, well. This is what I'm for, he thought. The day Romen came to stay he knew he had to protect him. From bad cops, street slaughter, dope death, prison shivs, and friendly fire in white folks' wars. He never would have believed a female would be a serious threat and his first real danger.

So he and Vida planned a way for him to be alone with his grandson. To his surprise the boy was as eager as he was. Did he want to talk too?

Vida stood at the window wiping her palms

together—a gesture of accomplishment. See-ing her husband and grandson drive off together on an errand soothed her. Romen's generation made her nervous. Nothing learned from her own childhood or from raising Dolly worked with them, and everywhere parents were flummoxed. These days the first thought at Christmas was the children; in her own gen-eration it was the last. Now children wept if their birthdays weren't banquets; then the day was barely acknowledged. The hardship stories told by her parents that mesmerized and steeled her made Romen cover his mouth to disguise a yawn. The gap was certainly normal now, but it wasn't eternal. That kid who threw a bucket of offal on Bill Cosey was not alone. Many had cheered.

Laughter and applause had interrupted the singing that furnace-hot afternoon. Cosey had been repairing a fishing rod in back of the hotel. Casting, rewinding, casting again, and then walking around to the front to see what the commotion was; to listen, perhaps, to the singing, or read the signs held aloft, some pleading, some demanding. As he approached, rod in hand, it looked to somebody like an excuse to raise the level from persuasion to argument to a drama carefully prepared for. A kid leapt forward with a pail and tossed its contents on Bill Cosey. The cheering subsided as Cosey remained where he was, animal waste spattering his shoes and trousers. He didn't move, not even to examine the soiling. Instead he looked at each one as though photographing them. Then he leaned the fishing rod against the porch railing and walked toward them. Slowly.

"Hey, Bella. Afternoon, Miss Barnes. Good to see you, George; got that truck running yet?"

He spoke to young and older. "How you doin', Pete? Your girl still in college? You looking good, Francie. Hi there, Shoofly . . ."

Courteous replies met his greetings and countered the violent smell of dung clotted on his cuffs and paving his way. Finally he raised his hand in a general farewell and left them as though he'd been inaugurated or baptized. The crowd lingered, but in disarray. Such was the rift between generations in 1968, but Cosey had managed to span it, to detox it; to say "I am neither stranger nor enemy." Talk, then, respectful but serious, was the bridge. Otherwise hog shit filled the gap. He never did what they were asking—give over some land—but he did try. Vida didn't know if it was May or Heed who prevented it, but she was thankful somebody had. Housing was more important than pottery classes. What would they be now? Homeless tai chi experts, miseducated vagabonds raising their children in condemned buildings and flatbed trucks. The choice, she thought, was not whether to surrender to power or dislodge it. It was to do your duty to your family, and at the moment, that meant serious talk to a grandson. Vida believed Romen had a natural tendency to care for people, but he seemed, nowadays, not to know what to do with it.

Fifteen aluminum-foiled platters were stacked on newspaper in the backseat, a name taped to each one. The list of shut-ins Vida had clipped to the visor included addresses, as though he might forget that Alice Brent was rooming now; that Mr. Royce had moved in with his daughter, who worked nights. Or that Miss Coleman, still on crutches, was staying with her blind brother on Governor Street. The shut-ins had three choices: fish, chicken, or barbecue, and the conflagration of aromas changed his car from a machine to a kitchen where talk could be easy.

Romen turned the radio on soon as he slid in, fiddling the buttons until he found what he liked: the music Vida made him wear head-phones to hear at home. That way only the throb and Romen's listening face disturbed her—not the words. Sandler liked the music but agreed with his wife that, unlike the suggestive language of their own generation ("I want some seafood, mama. Chicken and rice are very nice but gimme seafood, mama"), the language of Romen's music had the subtlety of an oil spill. "Polluting and disfiguring the natural mind," said Vida. Sandler reached over and turned the knob to "Off." He expected a whine from Romen, but none came. They rode in silence until he arrived at the first house on the list. Sandler had to pull the hands of three children away from his trousers to get to the front door. Alice Brent insisted on inviting him in, relinquishing the idea only when he told her she was first but he had fourteen deliveries left. Flattered, she let him go. He heard Romen click the radio back off, too late for Sandler not to notice. At least he respects my preference, he thought. Pulling away from the curb, he tried to think of some small talk. Something they could share before the interrogation or the lecture began. He and Vida had no son. Dolly, a sweet-tempered, obedient child, directed whatever rebellion she felt first into an early marriage, then into the armed forces. But it couldn't be that hard. Sandler's own father and grandfather had no trouble telling him what to do. Short, biting commands: "Never carry a lazy man's load," when he hauled too much at once in order to save himself frequent trips. "If she don't respect herself she won't respect you," or "Don't hang your pants where you can't hang your hat," when he claimed a quick conquest. No long sermons and no talking back. None of that worked with Romen. Sulk was the result of Sandler's efforts along those lines. Nineties children didn't want to hear "sayings" or be managed by lessons too dusty to be read, let alone understood. They got better advice from their hammering music. Straight no chaser. Black no sugar. Direct as a bullet.

"She pregnant?"

Romen was startled but not angry or evasive. "No! Why you ask me that?"

Good, thought Sandler. Direct like his own father but minus the threat. "Because you spend an awful lot of time with her. Doing what?"

"Just stuff."

"What stuff?"

"Ride around, you know," said Romen. "Went out to that old hotel last Saturday. Just looking around." For a floor, a pallet, anything would do as long as it was in a strange place. His palms were wet with excitement because she insisted he drive. Not just because he didn't know how but also because she liked to nuzzle and distract him while he struggled to control the wheel, and for the thrill of nearly hitting a tree or skidding into a ditch while fingering each other.

"You got in there?" asked Sandler.

"Yeah. It was open." The padlocked doors, the windows tight as iron so angered Romen he rammed his fist into a pane, matching the determination of Junior's hand in his jeans. They had thought the place would be scary: cobwebs and garbage-y corners. Instead, the kitchen, glowing in noon light, welcomed them to its tabletop as well as between its legs. Other rooms were dim but no less promising. Junior counted each as they explored themselves in every one, all the way from the lobby to the top floor.

"I don't believe anybody's been in there for years. Must be rat casino," Sandler said.

"Sorta." No rats. Birds. Flying and tittering in the rafters. The whole place smelled like wine.

"I take it they didn't get in your way?"

"No. I mean. We were just looking, fooling around, you know?"

"Who you think you talking to?"

"No, like, I mean—"

"Romen, we men or not?"

Romen looked at his high-tops. Black canvas with a cool white circle.

"Okay, then. Get off it. Straight, now."

"Okay. Well. She likes, she likes to . . ." Romen rubbed his knees.

"And you don't?"

"Aw, you know how it is."

"What happened?"

"Nothing. I mean, yeah. We made out and, like, explored everywhere. No big deal." Except for the attic. Getting up there required hoisting himself on a chair to get to the chain to pull down the folded stairs and climb in there. "We need matches," he told her, "or a flashlight." "No we don't," she whispered. "I like it dark." A rustle of wings and twitter as they entered. Bats? he wondered, but the wings that flew past, shooting through the hall light filtering into the attic, were yellow and he was about to say "Wow, canaries" when she pulled him to her. It was hide-and-seek then, tearing through spiderweb trellises. Losing, then finding each other in a pitch-black room; stumbling, bumping heads, tripping, falling, grabbing a foot, a neck, then the whole person, they dared darkness with loud laughter and moans of pleasure and pain. Birds screeched. Cartons toppled and crashed. Floorboards creaked, then split beneath them, raking their nakedness and sharpening their play, lending it a high seriousness he could never have imagined.

"No big deal?"

"Well, it did get, you know. Rough, I guess you'd say. Know what I mean?" He pushed—no, slammed—her against the wall after she squeezed his privates—and she had groaned happily instead of crying out when he bit her nipple, hard. It shifted then. From black to red. It was as though outside, looking on, he could see himself clearly in the dark—his bruised sweaty skin, his glittering teeth and half-closed eyes.

"What did you do, Romen? Out with it."

"Not me. Her."

"Will you just say it, boy?"

"She plays hard, that's all. I mean she likes being hurt."

Sandler braked at an intersection. It was a moment before he realized he had stopped at a green light. Romen was looking through the passenger window, waiting for some response, some grown-man comment worthy of his trust, his confidence, an answer to the question coiled in his confession. A chuckle from his grandfather would mean one thing. Reproach would mean another thing. Was there anything else? The traffic light changed.

"What do you think about that?" Sandler drove slowly through the red light pretending to be searching for an address.

"Weird. Wack." She didn't just like it. She preferred it. But the rush was in him as well. Standing next to himself, cold, unsmiling, watching himself inflict and suffer pain above scream level where a fresh kind of joy lay, the Romen who could not bear mittens laced to a bedpost, purple polish on bitten nails, the mud and vegetable smell of pulling bodies—that Romen evaporated. Never to be seen again, he was certain. Not in full, anyway. Just a faded version who, afterwards, felt annoyance instead of shame. Driving away from the hotel, he complained ("Chill, girl. Stop it. You going to make me have a wreck") about her leg banging his, the tip of her tongue on his neck, nipples pushed into his ear. Then there was the other thing. For the first time Junior had taken off her boots *and* her socks. When they had undressed back in the kitchen, as usual she kept her socks on. In the attic she removed them, tying one tightly around his neck. He was halfway down the attic ladder when he looked up. Junior, sitting in the opening, had the other one on. He couldn't be sure—light in the hall was scarce—but the foot she slipped into the sock looked to him like a hoof.

"Whack, huh? Well, I never believed much in free will. It ain't nothing if there's nothing you can control." Sandler parked in front of a pale blue house. The grass in front was patchy, starved for rain. "But of the few things you do have some say over, who you choose to hang out with is one. Looks like you hooked yourself up with somebody who bothers you, makes you feel uneasy. That kind of feeling is more than instinct; it's information, information you can count on. You can't always pay attention to what other people say, but you should pay attention to that. Don't worry about whether backing off means you a wimp. It can save your life. You not helpless, Romen. Don't ever think that. Sometimes it takes more guts to quit than to keep on. Some friends you know better than to bring home. There's a good reason for that, you understand me?"

"Yes, sir. I hear you."

"A woman is an important somebody and sometimes you win the triple crown: good food, good sex, and good talk. Most men settle for any one, happy as a clam if they get two. But listen, let me tell you something. A good man is a good thing, but there is nothing in the world better than a good good woman. She can be your mother, your wife, your girlfriend, your sister, or somebody you work next to.

Don't matter. You find one, stay there. You see a scary one, make tracks."

"I got you," said Romen.

The platters were cold but still savory and Sandler's mood was cheerful as they completed the deliveries. Romen was eager to help, jumping out first at each stop, lifting trays like a waiter as he trotted to the doors. Vida would be pleased. Don't fret, he'd tell her. Relax. He glanced at his grandson, who had not turned on the radio, just lay back on the headrest, asleep.

Romen, eyes closed, swallowed the saliva gathering in his mouth in anticipation of Junior's. Just talking about her turned him on. No matter what bothered him, she knocked him out. More than at first, when she was the starter. Now with the tender mixed with the rough, the trite language of desire smithereened by obscenities, he was the one in charge. He could beat her up if he wanted to and she would still go down. Funny. She was like a gorgeous pet. Feed it or whip it—it lapped you anyway.

The radio and tape player was for herself. The short-handled sponge mop was for Heed. So was the hairbrush with bristles finer than

Heed's other one. Junior spread the purchases on the dining room table. Heed might not appreciate the brush, but she would love the convenience of the little mop for personal hygiene. It even had a wrist loop so it wouldn't slip from hands that don't work properly. The best thing, thought Junior, was to convince her to get out of that tub and into a shower. Have a little seat put in there. Safer. Easier. Get her to have two showers installed—one for the second floor as well. All that cash and nothing to spend it on. Locking herself in at night, going nowhere in the day. Now she wanted to be driven out to the hotel, in secret. Neither Heed nor Christine paid any attention to the rest of the house—what was needed in it. The dining room, big, never used, should be done over. Get rid of the ceiling fan, the ugly table. Put in some sofas, chairs, a television. Junior smiled, realizing she was turning the space into Correctional's Rec Room. Well, why not? And the living room, too, needed help. It had a rerun look, like a house in an old TV show with loud rich kids and talky parents. She walked across the hall and sat on the living room sofa. A sectional, turquoise on once-white carpeting. The glittery pear-shaped lamps on the end tables were both cracked. Two panels of striped drapes sagged from their rods; others were ripped. Battle signs, she thought. Before they got too old or tired to do it anymore and settled for unsmashable silence.

Sitting there, Junior felt the kick of being, living, in a house, a real house, her first. A place with different reasons for each room and different things to put in them. She wondered what her Good Man liked. Velvet? Wicker? Had he picked this stuff? Did he even care? You didn't like it here, did you? Who broke the lamps? Who glued them back—Christine? Was it Heed who grabbed the drapes? She talks about you all the time. About how she adored you, but she's faking it, right? And Christine hates you. Your eyes are smiling in your picture but your mouth looks hungry. You married an eleven-year-old girl. I ran away when I was eleven. They brought me back, then put me in Correctional. I had a G.I. Joe but they took it. If you'd known me then, nobody would have messed with me. You'd have taken care of me because you understand me and everything and won't let anybody get me. Did you marry Heed to protect her? Was that the only way? An Old Man tried to make me do things. Force me. I didn't, though. If you'd been there you'd have killed him. They said I tried to, but I didn't. Try to, I mean. I know you called me here. I read the ad in a paper I found in the bus station. It was lying right next to me on the bench. A long shot. I took two twenties from a woman's wallet. She left her purse on the sink when she went to the other end of the bathroom to dry her hands. I knocked her purse over and apologized. She didn't check. Terry loaned me some of her clothes. Kind of. I mean she would've loaned them if I'd asked her to. I met her in the Red Moon. Correctional gave me one hundred dollars for three years' work. I spent it in movies and restaurants. Terry waitressed at the Red Moon. We got on; laughed a lot. She invited me to stay over when I told her I was sleeping in daylight. Church pews, movies, in the sand near the piers. Moving all the time so Cops wouldn't see me and think I was drunk or on something. I never drink or do dope. It feels good but you miss a lot when your head is fucked. I don't want to miss anything, anything at all. Being locked away all those years. My fault, I guess. I was fifteen and on my way out. I should have known. But I only knew Boys, not Men. Do you like my Boyfriend? He's beautiful, isn't he? So nice and mean. Who has legs like that? His shoulders are a mile wide and they don't move when he walks. God. I want to keep him, okay? He was late today because he had to be with his Grandfather. It was ice cold in the garage, but we fucked anyway eating barbecue. You should have seen us. But you did, didn't you? You go wherever you want and I know you liked the hotel better than here. I can tell when me and my Boyfriend go there. I feel you all over the place. Heed wants me to do something in there. She won't tell me what, but I know it's something to fix Christine for good. Dream on. The game they're playing? Both lose. I just have to make sure it's not me. Or you. I don't know why I said that. Sorry. I'm still not used to it. Sometimes I forget you're my Good Man.

8

FATHER

The hiking boots, purchased with Anna Krieg's instruction, are what she needs. The road to the hotel is treacherous for a hysterical pedestrian on a chilly night in tennis shoes and no socks. The tough-minded Anna Krieg would have been prepared: rucksack, water, flashlight, *brot,* dried fish, nuts. Christine had learned how to cook from her while they both, wives of American soldiers, were stationed in Germany. Barely twenty, devoted to the PX, Anna was adept with fresh vegetables, varieties of potatoes, seafood, but especially voluptuous desserts. Cooking lessons and beer made the evenings cheery and postponed the collapse of Christine's marriage into a desolation exactly like the quarters they lived in. In return for the friendship, Christine agreed one day to hike with Anna. She bought the good boots and rucksack Anna recommended and early one morning they set out. Halfway to the halfway point, Christine stopped and begged to cancel, to hitch back to the base. Her feet were on fire; her lungs hyphenating. Anna's face registered extreme disappointment but understanding too. "Poor, soft American, no stamina, no will." They turned back in silence.

When Christine opened the door she found Ernie locked in the arms of the staff sergeant's wife. She wanted to kick his bare behind, but her feet hurt so she settled for six bottles of Spaten hurled in rapid succession at his head.

For the benefit and morale of the other wives in this newly desegregated army, she felt obliged to go through the motions of jealous rage, but she was more dumbfounded than angry. Puzzled as to who Ernie Holder thought he was, other than a raggedy Pfc. who had offered devotion, a uniform, and escape to another country in exchange for her own gorgeous well-bred self. She left him the next day, taking rucksack, cooking skills, and hiking boots with her. From Idlewild, she called her mother. May seemed relieved to hear her voice but ambivalent about her return to Silk. Her jumbled chatter held no curiosity about Christine's situation but was spiked instead with references to the "swamp wife" and a burned "freedom" bus. Clearly she was being warned away.

Since the atmosphere May described seemed so dank and small-town-y, Christine lingered. After two nights not quite on the street (a bus station didn't count), after being turned away from the YWCA, she moved into a Phillis Wheatley House. The country, so joyful and pleased with itself when she'd left it, was frightened now by red threats and blacklists. On looks alone she got a job in a restaurant waitressing until they discovered she could cook. It was a friendly neighborhood place where she laughed at the ways customers found to hustle free food, and where she spent years avoiding and lying to May while searching for a husband. She had found three, none her own, when she met Fruit. By then she was steeped in and bored by workplace gossip involving the owner, his wife, the cashier, and the short-order cook. The pointless malice exhausted her, as did the drift of conversation between herself and whatever married man she was attached to. She didn't really care whether he separated from his wife or not, slept with the mother of his children or not, gave her a lesser Christmas present or not. But since they never had friends in common, there was nothing else to talk about except proofs of affection and threats of dissolution. It was an outline of a life, a doodling on a paper napkin yet to be filled in while she purposely stayed away from the home May described. Into that aimlessness came Fruit, with a canvas satchel and a flawlessly ironed work shirt.

"Don't hide the meat. I like to see what I eat." Christine withheld the red gravy and wondered at his clarity—which she discovered later was his habit and his gift. When she listened to him, everything was suddenly so clear she spent nine years in his company. He was a fine-boned man, intense, with large beautiful hands and a mesmerizing voice. He clarified the world for her. Her grandfather (a bourgeois traitor); her mother (a handkerchief-head); Heed (a field hand wannabe); Ernie (a sellout). They were the "chumps" Malcolm X described, acid dripping from the word. Then he outlined her own obligations. With apology for her light skin, gray eyes, and hair threatening a lethal silkiness, Christine became a dedicated helpmate, coherent and happy to serve. She changed her clothing to "motherland," sharpened her language to activate slogans, carried a knife for defense, hid her inauthentic hair in exquisite gelés; hung cowrie shells from her earlobes, and never crossed her legs at the knees.

Her fears that she might disappoint such a man, fierce, uncorruptible, demanding, or that he might be forced to treat her like dirt were never realized because Fruit liked dirt. His view of soil, earth, crops was a romance he shared with her. A farm, he said, if we had one, it could be a base for us. Christine agreed, but events were so swift and money (collected, wheedled, extorted) was needed for other emergencies.

All over the country there were sleeping neighborhoods that needed arousing, inattentive young people needing focus. The hiking boots were broken in at marches; her rucksack simulated comfort at sit-ins. Pumped by seething exhilaration and purpose, Christine's personal vanity became racial legitimacy and her flair for acting out became courage. She hardly remembered the quarrels now: informants galore, tainted money, random acts vs. long-range plans, underground vs. dance with the media. Theirs was a group of seventeen— eleven black, six white—an underground formed after the Till trial. Independent, autonomous, they joined other groups only when they judged the activity strong enough.

She relished the work; thrived on its seriousness and was totally committed to Fruit. There,
with him, she was not in the way; she was in.
Not the disrupting wife, the surplus mistress,
the unwanted nuisance daughter, the ignored
granddaughter, the disposable friend. She was
valuable. There was no reason why it could not
last. The urgency planted in 1955 had blossomed in 1965, and was ripe with fury in
1968. By 1970, sapped by funerals, it seemed to
wane for her. Nina Simone helped delay the
beginning of the end. That voice lent status to
female surrender, and romance to blunt trans-
gression. So when the end arrived, it was
unrecognizable as such. A small, quite insignif-
icant toilet flush. After a routine abortion, the
last of seven, she rose, tapped the lever, and
turned to watch the swirl. There, in a blur of
congealed red, she thought she saw a profile.
For less than a second that completely impossible image surfaced. Christine bathed and
went back to bed. She had always been unsen-
timental about abortions, considering them as
one less link in the holding chain, and she did
not want to be a mother—ever. Besides, no
one stopped her or suggested she do otherwise: Revolutions needed men—not fathers.
So this seventh intervention did not trouble
her in the least. Although she realized she had

conjured up the unborn eye that had disappeared in a cloud of raspberry red, still, on
occasion, she wondered who it was who
looked up at her with such quiet interest. At
the oddest moments—cloistered in a hospital
waiting room with a shot boy's weeping
mother, dispensing bottled water and raisins to
exhausted students—that noncommittal eye
seemed to be there, at home in the chaos of
cops and tears. Had she paid closer attention,
perhaps she could have stalled, even prevented,
the real end, but her grandfather died. Fruit
encouraged her to attend the funeral (family is
family, he said, smiling, even if they are politi-
cal morons). Christine hesitated. She would
have to be in Heed's murderous company; her
mother and she would continue to argue politics as they did during intermittent phone
calls, screaming accusations: Why can't you all
just quiet down? Three hundred years of quiet
not enough for you? We'll lose everything! All
we slaved for! SLAM.

He was dead. The dirty one who intro-
duced her to nasty and blamed it on her.

He was dead. The powerful one who abandoned his own kin and transferred rule to her
playmate.

He was dead. Well, good. She would go and
view the wreck he left behind.

Nothing is watching now. It is long gone, the nonjudgmental eye, along with the rucksack and the hiking boots which she desperately needs now if she is going to stop the snake and her minion from destroying the balance of her life. The two of them, Heed and Junior, were nowhere in the house. The garage was empty, the driveway clear. Nothing could make Heed leave her room but devilment—and at night? There is only one place she could be interested in—the hotel—and there was no time to waste even if she had to run all the way.

No one could have guessed, but Fruit was eight years younger than she was, so of course he pleased himself with other women. That was the beauty, the honesty of their relationship. She of all people, queen of seduced husbands, understood, having grown up in a hotel where the tippy-toe of bare feet, the rustle behind the equipment shed, the eye-blaze of one female guest aimed at another had been everyday stuff. Hadn't she heard her grandfather tell his wife in front of everybody, "Don't wag your little tail at me. I don't want it and I sure don't need it," and leave that wife dancing alone at the birthday party while he raced off to meet whoever it was he did need? Notwithstanding Ernie Holder and the Spaten

soaring toward his head, having men meant
sharing them. Get used to it and do it with
grace, right? Other women's beds were not a
problem. Anyway, with all the work to be
done, who had time to monitor every stray
coupling? She was the designated woman, the
one everybody acknowledged as such. Their
names spoken in a planning meeting sounded
like a candy bar: Fruit 'n' Chris. Chris 'n' Fruit.

The candy bar didn't crumble until somebody raped one of the student volunteers. A
Comrade had done it. The girl, too ashamed to
be angry, begged Christine not to tell her
father, a university dean.

"Please, please don't."

"What about your mother?"

"Oh no! She'll tell *him*!"

Christine bristled. Like a Doberman puppy
in training, the girl had gone into protection
mode. Good Daddy Big Man mustn't know.
Christine ignored her, told everyone, and was
satisfied especially by Fruit's response. They all
took care of the girl, cursed and fumed at what
the Comrade had done; promised to speak to,
punish, expel him. But didn't. The next time
he showed up, it was "Hey, man, how's it
going?" When Christine cornered Fruit he
reported what the Comrade had said: it wasn't
his fault the girl was all over him braless sitting

sloppy he'd even patted her behind to alert her to his interest she giggled instead of breaking his jaw and asked him if he wanted a beer. Fruit shook his head, mourning human stupidity and retrograde politics. Yet mourn was all he did. Regardless of her urging, "speaking to"—not to mention "punish" or "expel"—he never got around to. Yes, Fruit thought the Comrade a menace, but he could not tell him so. Yes, he believed the Comrade jeopardized their principled cause, but he could not confront him. The girl's violation carried no weight against the sturdier violation of male friendship. Fruit could upbraid, expel, beat up a traitor, a coward, or any jive turkey over the slightest offense. But not this one—this assault against a girl of seventeen was not even a hastily added footnote to his list of Unacceptable Behavior since the raped one did not belong to him. Christine did the racial equation: the rapee is black and the raper white; both are black; both are white. Which combination influenced Fruit's decision? It would have helped if the other girls' moans of sympathy for the raped one had not been laced with disturbing questions: What did *she* do? Why didn't *she* . . . ?

Eventually Christine shut up about it and the good work of civil disobedience and personal obedience went on, interrupted only now and then by the profile, turning, offering its uncritical eye. When she got back from her grandfather's funeral, she opened her rucksack and shook out the paper bag of engagement rings. Solitaires of all sizes. Enough to get twelve women to sign the guest book at Hotel Make-Believe. The question apparently was how comfortable is the suite? In 1973 Tremaine Avenue, with its high level of comfort, was mighty attractive. Especially since everybody, militants and moderates, wanted to be in and stay out at the same time, the good work of disobedience was merging with disguised acquiescence. The issues changed, spread, moved from streets and doorways to offices and conferences in elegant hotels. Nobody needed a street-worker-baby-sitter-cook-mimeographing-marching-nut-and raisin-carrying woman who was too old anyway for the hip new students with complex strategies; a woman not educated enough for the college crowd, not shallow enough for television. The disinterested eye, carefully studied by the Supreme Court, had closed. She was irrelevant. Fruit sensed her despair and they parted as friends.

He was, she thinks, the last true friend she had. He would have mourned again if he knew what she had settled for: kept woman to a mimeographed copy of her bourgeois grandfather. And rightly, for after Dr. Rio threw her out there was no place like and no place but home. Hers. To hang on to and keep an insane viper from evicting her.

Christine was in a car the last time she traveled this road. Up front, too, because her wide skirts—a powder-blue heap of chiffon—need room. She is wearing a movie star's gown, strapless with rhinestones sprinkling the top. Her mother is in the backseat; her grandfather is driving the 1939 Pontiac, which irritates him because it is already 1947 and postwar cars are still unavailable to most civilians. That is what he is saying, explaining his strange mood at a time of giddy celebration: Christine's delayed sixteenth-birthday and graduation party. She thinks the real reason he is agitated is the same reason she and her mother are jubilant. At the family-only dinner preceding the hotel party, they have managed to eliminate Heed and have had the pleasure of watching her disciplined by her husband. At last, just the three of them. No ignorant, clinging wifelet to sully this magnificent homecoming display.

Christine, led from the car on her grandfather's arm, makes a glamorous entrance; an Oh-so-pretty-girl-in-perfectly-beautiful gown, proof and consequence of racial uplift and proper dreams. The band plays "Happy Birthday" over the crowd's applause, then segues into "Harbor Lights." May beams. Christine glows. The hotel is packed with uniformed veterans, vacationing couples, and Cosey's friends. The musicians switch to "How High the Moon," since the future is not just bright, it is there, visible in paychecks, tangible in G.I. Bill applications, audible in the scat vocalist's range. Just look through the wide doors beyond the open-air dance floor and see the way the stars go. Hear the waves roll; inhale the ocean's cologne, how sweet and male it is.

Then a flutter, a murmur of disbelief. Turning heads. Heed is in the center of the room dancing with a man in a green zoot suit. He lifts her over his head, brings her down between his legs, casts her aside, splits, and rises on angled legs in time to meet her hips shimmying toward his clenched pelvis. The band blasts. The crowd parts. Bill Cosey places his napkin on the table and stands. The guests look sideways at his approach. Zoot suit halts mid-step, his pocket chain swung low. Heed's dress looks like a red slip; the shoulder strap falls to her elbow. Bill Cosey doesn't look at the man, shout, or pull Heed away. In fact he does not touch her. The musicians, alert to every nuance of crowd drama, grow silent, so everybody hears Bill Cosey's dismissal and his remedy.

The crash of the sea is sounding in Christine's ears. She is not close enough to the shore to hear it, so this must be heightened blood pressure. Next will come the dizziness and zigzags of light before her eyes. She should rest a moment, but Heed is not resting. Heed is doing something secret with an able-bodied spider to help her.

She should have known. She did know. Junior had no past, no history but her own. The things she didn't know about or had never heard of would make a universe. The minute the girl sat down at the kitchen table lacing her lies with Yes, ma'ams, oozing street flavor like a yell, she knew: This girl will do anything. Yet that was precisely what was so appealing. And you had to admire any girl who survived on the street without a gun. The bold eyes, the mischievous smile. Her willingness to do any errand, tackle any difficulty, was a blessing for Christine. But more than that, Junior listened. To complaints, jokes, justifications, advice, reminiscences. Never accusing, judging—simply interested. In that silent house talking to anybody was like music. Who cared if she sneaked around with Vida's grandson from time to time? Good for him. Fun for her. A happily sexed girl would be more likely to stay on. What Christine had forgotten was the runaway's creed: Hang in, hang out, hang loose. Meaning friendship, yes. Loyalty, no.

The hotel is darker than the night. No lights, but the car is parked in the driveway. No voices either. The ocean is whispering underneath the blood roaring in her ears. Maybe this is a lure. Maybe she will open the door and they will kill her, as they would not Anna Kreig, who would have had the sense not to bolt out of a house in tennis shoes and no Swiss Army knife. Stumbling along in the dark, she has seldom felt more alone. This is like the time she first learned how sudden, how profound, loneliness could be. She was five when her father died. One Saturday he gave her a baseball cap, the following Monday they carried him down the stairs on a metal stretcher. His eyes were half closed and he didn't answer when she called him. People kept coming and coming to comfort the parent, the widow; kept whispering about how hard it was to lose a son, a husband, a friend. Nothing was said about the loss of a father. They simply patted her on the head and smiled. That was the first time she took refuge under L's bed, and if she had her druthers, she would be there now instead of climbing toward the place that rocked her with fear and, and—what was the other thing? Oh, yes. Sorrow.

Christine gazes into the darkness huddling the porch steps where a sunlit child is rigid with fear and the grief of abandonment. Yet her hand raised in farewell is limp. Only the bow in her hair is more languid than that hand. Beyond her gaze is another child, staring through the window of an automobile, idling, purring like a cat. The driver is the grandfather of one, the husband of the other. The passenger's face is a blend of wild eyes, grin, and confusion. The limp hand waves while the other one's fingers press the car window. Will it break? Will her fingers crack the glass, cutting the skin and spilling blood down the side of the door? They might, because she is pressing so hard. Her eyes are large, but she is grinning too. Does she want to go? Is she afraid to go? Neither one understands. Why can't she go too? Why is he taking one to a honeymoon and leaving the other? They will come back, won't they? But when? She looks so alone in that big car, but she is smiling—or trying to. There ought to be blood. There must be blood somewhere, because the sunlit child on the porch is holding herself stiff against the possibility. Only her farewell hand is soft, limp. Like the bow in her hair.

A thorn of pain scratches Christine's shoulder as she climbs the steps. She reaches through the dark for the doorknob. She can't find it. The door is open.

"You sure you want to do this? We can go back." Junior leaves the motor running. Her exquisite nose ring flickers in the late sun. "Or tell me what to look for and you stay here." She is nervous. Her Good Man hasn't shown up for some time. She hopes he is here in the hotel. Everything is going fine, but it would be nicer if he were around to say so. "We can do this some other day. Anytime you want to. It's up to you, though."

Heed is not listening. Neither is she looking through a car window at a ruined hotel in twilight. She is twenty-eight years old, standing at its second-floor window facing the lawn and, beyond that, sand and sea. Beneath her, women and children look like butterflies flitting in and out of the tents. The men wear white shirts, black suits. The preacher is in a rocking chair;

he keeps his straw hat on. More and more she rents to churches, groups. Former guests, older now, don't return to Cosey's Resort often. Their children are preoccupied with boycotts, legislation, voting rights. A mother sits apart, a white handkerchief over her nursing breast. One hand holds the baby, the other slowly fanning in case a fly soars near. She could have had children too, Heed is thinking. Would have had them if she had known in 1942 what one slip into another man's arms taught her in 1958: that she wasn't barren at all. The man— he came to collect his brother's body, accompany it on the train back home. Heed, remembering the pain of losing two brothers, tells him that his room, as long as he likes, will be free. And if there is anything else she can do . . . He sat on the bed and wept. She touched his shoulder rising and falling in unmanageable grief. She had never seen a sober man cry. Heed knelt down, gazing at the hand covering his eyes, and took the one on his knee. His fingers clutched hers and they held that position until he quieted.

"Sorry. I'm sorry," he said, reaching for his handkerchief.

"Don't be. Don't never be sorry for crying over somebody." She was almost shouting and he looked at her as though she had said the smartest thing ever heard.

"You need to eat something," she said. "I'll bring you a tray. Anything special you want?"

He shook his head. "Anything."

She ran downstairs, suddenly aware of the difference between being needed and being obliged. In the kitchen she prepared a roast pork sandwich and swaddled the meat in hot sauce. Thinking of the adorable paunch pushing out his shirt, she added a bottle of beer as well as ice water to the tray. L looked askance at the food, so Heed answered her unasked question. "It's for the dead man's brother."

"Did I use too much?" she asked when he bit into the sandwich.

He shook his head. "Perfect. How did you know?"

Heed laughed. "Mr. Sinclair, you let me know directly if you need something. Anything at all."

"Knox. Please."

"I'm Heed," she said, thinking, I have to get out of this room or I'll kiss his belly.

Knox Sinclair stayed six days, the length of time needed to arrange for, prepare, then ship the body to Indiana. Each day was more glorious than the one before. Heed helped him with telephone calls, telegraphed money, trips to Harbor for the death certificate. Tended him with the care any good hotel manager who had a guest drown would.

That was the excuse. The reason was Jimmy Witherspoon singing "Ain't nobody's business if I do." She got her wish and was able to nestle and stroke his belly nightly while her husband entertained clientele, and in the morning while he slept it off. She made Knox talk about his brother, his life, just to hear his northern accent. She was stunned to be wanted by a man her own age who found her interesting, intelligent, desirable. So this is what happy feels like.

"Forever" is what they promised each other. He will return in six weeks and they will go away together. For six weeks Papa's fishing "parties" were a relief, his night murmurs pathetic. She planned so carefully even L didn't catch on: new clothes packed away in two suitcases; the till modestly but regularly raided.

He never showed.

She called his house in Indiana. A woman answered. Heed hung up. Called again and spoke to her.

"Is this the Sinclair residence?"

"Yes, it is." A warm voice, kind.

"May I speak to Mr. Sinclair, please?"

"I'm sorry. He's not here. Would you like to leave a message?"

"No. Bye. I mean, thanks."

Another call. The warm voice answers, "This is Mrs. Sinclair. Can I help you?"

"I'm Mrs. Cosey. From the hotel where Mr. Sinclair uh stayed."

"Oh. Is there a problem?"

"No. Uh. You his wife?"

"Whose wife?"

"Knox. Knox Sinclair, I mean."

"Oh, no dear. I'm his mother."

"Oh. Well. Would you tell him, have him call me? Mrs. Cosey at . . ."

He didn't and Heed called seven times more until his mother said, "I've lost a son, dear. He's lost a brother. Please don't call here again."

Her badly smashed heart was quickly mended when she learned, after fifteen years of questions and pity, that she was pregnant. Sorry as she was about "not here" Knox, she would trade a father for a child any day. Gleaming in anticipation, she felt kind, generous. Unique but not isolated; important without having to prove it. When a single instance of spotting was followed by heavy clotting, she was not alarmed because her breasts continued to swell and her appetite remained ravenous.

Dr. Ralph reassured her everything was fine. Her weight gain was as sharp as May's looks, and steady, like Papa's smiles. She had no menses for eleven months and would have had none for eleven more if L had not sat her down, slapped her—hard—then peered into her eyes, saying, "Wake up, girl. Your oven's cold." After months of darkness thickened by public snigger and her husband's recoil, she did wake up and, skinny as a witch, rode into daylight on a broomstick.

The mother finishes nursing and rocks the baby on her shoulder. Back and forth. Back and forth. The church folk, drained of color by a rising moon, leave the lawn in small groups. Overfed. Calling out happy goodbyes.

Her baby was a son, she was sure, and had he been born she wouldn't need to sneak off, driven by an untethered teenager to a collapsing hotel in order to secure her place.

Taking out her key, Heed notices the broken pane in the door.

"Somebody's busted in here."

"Could be," says Junior. She opens the door.

Heed follows and waits while Junior rummages in her shopping bag of supplies: lightbulbs, scissors, pen, flashlight. It won't be dark for at least an hour, so they easily find their way to the third floor and the chain hanging from the attic hatch. There the flashlight is needed while Junior searches the ceiling for the fixture.

Standing on a crate, she screws in a bulb and pulls the string.

Heed is shocked. The attic's layout, indelible in her memory for decades, is blasted. Boxes are everywhere, in disarray, open, smashed, upside down. Bedsprings angled dangerously against broken chairs, rakes, carpet samples, stewing pots. Disoriented, Heed twirls, saying, "I told you somebody busted in here. Trying to steal from me."

"Kids maybe," says Junior. "Fooling around."

"How you know? Anything could be missing. Look at this mess. This is going to take all night." Heed stares at a rusty electric fan. Her nerves are strung.

"What are we looking for?" Junior speaks softly, trying to soothe her, thinking, We must have scared off the birds. Not a single one twittered.

"Rinso," Heed snaps. "A big old box with R-I-N-S-O on it. It's here somewhere."

"Well," says Junior, "let's get started."

"I can't get around this mess."

"Wait here." Junior drags and hauls until a path, front to back, is cleared. Over cracked and slanting floorboards she tosses a yard of flowered carpet and rights a carton of men's shoes. Cobwebs are not a problem.

While they search, Junior smells baking bread, something with cinnamon. "You smell something?" she asks.

Heed sniffs. "Smells like L," she says.

"Hell can't smell that good," answers Junior.

Heed lets it go.

"There! Look!" Junior points. "It's behind you. Up there."

Heed turns to look. osniR. "That don't say Rinso."

"It's upside down." Junior laughs.

Heed is embarrassed. "Must be losing my sight," she says. Suddenly Junior is annoying. What's that look? Mocking? Disrespectful? "Over here," she directs, pointing to where she wants Junior to place the carton.

Finally situated, cartons for seats, chair for desk, Heed thumbs through a bundle of menus. Most have only the month and day, but several show the year: 1964. She is about to instruct Junior what to write in the spaces when she notices the ballpoint pen in Junior's fingers.

"What's that? I said a fountain pen. He wouldn't use that. He wouldn't use nothing but real ink. Oh Lord, you messing this whole thing up. I told you! Didn't I tell you?"

Junior lowers her eyes, thinking what the fuck is the matter with her who does she think she is I'm helping her steal or trick or lie and she talks to me like a warden? Saying,

"In 1964 he might have."

"No he wouldn't. You don't know what you talking about."

"Well, a ballpoint proves it's more recent, doesn't it? A later version," idiot.

"You think?"

"Sure," you ignorant bitch.

"Maybe you right. Okay. Here's what you say." Heed closes her eyes and dictates. "I leave all my wordly good to my dear wife Heed the Night . . ."

Junior looks up but doesn't say anything. It's clear why the Good Man stopped liking her— if he ever did. "Wordly good." Is he listening? Is he laughing? Is he here? She can't tell. The cinnamon bread is not him.

". . . who have stood by me faithful all these years. In case of her death, if she leaves no will her own self, everything goes to . . ." Heed pauses, smiles. "Solitude Johnson."

Yeah. Sure. Junior scribbles quickly. She has practiced her Good Man's handwriting to perfection. "Is that all?" she asks.

"Shh!"

"What?"

"I hear something." Heed's eyes widen.

"I don't."

"It's her."

"Christine? I don't hear anything."

"You wouldn't."

Heeds stands up, glancing around for something to use for protection. Nothing is available.

"Stop worrying," says Junior. "If she gets close, I'll—"

"Fool! She'll wipe the floor with you!" She snatches the pen from Junior and waits. Both hear the measured footsteps ascending the ladder. Both watch the crown, then the face rise into the light. The eyes are terrible. Christine enters the room and stands still. For breath ease? To decide? Junior breaks into the quiet.

"Oh, hi," she says. "How'd you get here? We were just looking some stuff up. For her book, remember? Dates have to be checked, right? That's what research is all about, they say."

If they hear her, they give no sign. Christine remains still; Heed is moving, cautiously taking one step, then another, the Bic clenched between palm and powerful thumb. The eyes of each are enslaved by the other's. Opening pangs of guilt, rage, fatigue, despair are replaced by a hatred so pure, so solemn, it feels beautiful, almost holy.

Junior's head tracks left to right, like a tennis fan's. She senses rather than sees where Heed, blind to everything but the motionless figure before her, is heading—one footfall at a time. Carefully, with the toe of her boot, Junior eases the piece of carpeting toward herself. She does not watch or call out. Instead, she turns to smile at Christine, whose blood roar is louder than the cracking, so the falling is like a silent movie and the soft twisted hands with no hope of hanging on to rotted wood dissolve, fade to black as movies always do, and the feeling of abandonment loosens a loneliness so intolerable that Christine drops to her knees peering down at the body arching below. She races down the ladder, along the hall, and into the room. On her knees again, she turns, then gathers Heed in her arms. In light sifting from above each searches the face of the other. The holy feeling is still alive, as is its purity, but it is altered now, overwhelmed by desire. Old, decrepit, yet sharp. The attic light goes out, and although they can hear boots running, the engine start of a car, they are neither surprised nor interested. There in a little girl's bedroom an obstinate skeleton stirs, clacks, refreshes itself.

The aroma of baking bread was too intense. Cinnamon-flavored. He wasn't there. Although Junior couldn't tell yet what he might be thinking, she was sure he would laugh when she told him, showed him the forged menu his airhead wife thought would work, and the revisions Junior had made in case it did. Sorry, Solitude. She pushed a little harder on the gas pedal. It was a long shot, sudden, unpremeditated, but it might turn out the way she dreamed. If either or both got out, she would say she fled to get help or something. But first she had to get to Monarch Street, find him, share the excitement and her smarts. She parked and ran down the steps. The kitchen door was wide open, swinging in icy air. Christine must have left not just in a hurry but in a fit. She hadn't turned the lights or the oven off, and a shriveled leg of lamb clung to its juices caramelizing in the pan. Junior turned the knob to "Off," then wandered the rooms, irritated by the odor of burnt meat hiding his cologne. He was nowhere, not even in his study, so she went directly to him. Good. There he was. Smiling welcome above Heed's bed. Her Good Man.

On Monarch Street Romen pedaled into the driveway. Leaning his bike on the garage door, he noticed steam coming from the Oldsmobile. He touched the hood. It was warm. When Junior answered his knock she seemed to him as beautiful as it is possible for a human to be. Her hair, like it was when he first saw her: soft, loud, mixing threat and invitation. The sci-fi eyes were bright and she was wearing smile number thirty-one. They made out where they stood and he did not think to ask where the women were until Junior led him up to the third-floor bedroom.

"Look what I got." Junior was propped in Heed's bed under the man's picture. Naked, waving a folded sheet of paper. Romen hadn't looked at it.

"Where's Mrs. Cosey? I never knew her to leave this room."

"Visiting her granddaughter," Junior laughed.

"What granddaughter?"

"Lives over in Harbor, she said."

"No kidding?"

"Come here." Junior yanked back the covers. "Take your clothes off and get in here."

"She'll catch us, girl."

"Not a chance. Come on!"

Romen didn't want to do it with that face hanging on the wall, so he pulled Junior into the bathroom, where they filled the tub to see what it was like underwater. Confining, he discovered; not as groovy as he thought it would be until they pretended to drown each other. They sloshed water and called each other filthy names until, like spent salmon, they fell apart, sucking air at opposite ends of the tub. He angled away from the spigot, she resting her head on the rim.

Feeling strong and melted at the same time, Romen reached under the water and raised Junior's misshapen foot above it. She flinched, tried to yank it out of his hands, but he held on and held on, looking closely at the mangled toes. Then, bending his head, he lifted them to his tongue. After a moment he felt her soften, give, so when he looked up he was surprised to see how dead her sci-fi eyes were.

Afterwards, beneath the covers in Heed's bed, he woke from a short nap and said, "Serious. Where are they?"

"At the hotel."

"What for?"

Junior told him then what had happened in the attic. She sounded like a TV newsreader, remote, faking lather about an incident of no importance.

"You left them there?"

"Why not?" She seemed genuinely surprised by his question. "Turn over. Let me lick your back."

"I hate that picture. Like screwing in front of your father." Her saliva was cool on his spine.

"Then turn out the light, sugarboy."

9

PHANTOM

Heed can't look. Christine has covered her feet, in perfect fourth position now, with a quilt and gone to search for something to ease the pain. There could be all sorts of items sequestered by May: liquor in a toilet tank, aspirin in a flue. Heed hopes for the first because there is no water and she would like to pass out from drunkenness rather than agony. Her bones, fragile from decades of stupor, have splintered like glass. The ankles are not the only joints she believes are cracked. There is a dullness in her pelvis and she can't lift her right leg. Christine has propped her against the wall since there is no mattress on the bed. In her wisdom, when the hotel closed, she sold everything possible.

Drawing a ribbon of breath, she blocks any tears that may be lurking like memories behind her eyelids. But the forget-me-nots roaming the wallpaper are more vivid in this deliberate dark than they ever were in daylight and she wonders what it was that made her want it so. Home, she thinks. When I stepped in the door, I thought I was home.

Christine's familiar tread interrupts her efforts to remember more. She has found things: among them matches, a box of hurricane candles, a can of Dole pineapple, and some packets of Stanback powder. She lights a candle, securing it in its own drippings. If she can manage to open the pineapple, Heed can swallow the powder. Wordlessness continues as Christine uses a ball peen to bang a stud nail into the rim of the can. When she succeeds, she opens two packets and sifts the bitter powder into Heed's mouth, alternating it with the juice. She pulls the quilt up around her shoulders because Heed is shivering.

They both had expected a quarrel. Who's to blame? Who started it all by hiring a thief and who made it necessary by consulting a lawyer? Whose fault is it they are abandoned seven miles from humanity with nobody knowing they are there or caring even if they do know?

No one is praying for them and they have never prayed for themselves. Still, they avoid rehearsing accusations, a waste of breath now with one of them cracked to pieces and the other sweating like a laundress. Up here where the solitude is like the room of a dead child, the ocean has no scent or roar. The future is disintegrating along with the past. The landscape beyond this room is without color. Just a bleak ridge of stone and no one to imagine it otherwise, because that is the way it is—as, deep down, everyone knows. An unborn world where sound, any sound—the scratch of a claw, the flap of webbed feet—is a gift. Where a human voice is the only miracle and the only necessity. Language, when finally it comes, has the vigor of a felon pardoned after twenty-one years on hold. Sudden, raw, stripped to its underwear.

You know May wasn't much of a mother to me.

At least she didn't sell you.

No, she gave me away.

Maple Valley?

Maple Valley.

I thought you wanted to go.

Hell no. But so what if I did? I was thirteen. She was the mama. She wanted me gone because he did, and she wanted whatever he wanted. Except you. She was Daddy's girl. Not you.

Don't I know it.

I bet she made your life a horror movie.

Her own too. For years I believed she was hiding stuff just to devil me. I didn't know it was Huey Newton she was scared of.

She thought the Panthers were after her?

Among others. She wanted to be ready. In case.

Yeah. For the real revolution: twenty-year-old boys fighting to bed sixty-year-old women.

They could do worse.

They did do worse.

You ever meet any?

No. I was out of it by then.

Was it worth it?

No question.

I called you a fool, but I was jealous too. The excitement and all.

It had that.

You sound sad.

No. It's just. Well, it's like we started out being sold, got free of it, then sold ourselves to the highest bidder.

Who you mean "we"? Black people? Women? You mean me and you?

I don't know what I mean. Christine touches Heed's ankle. The unswollen one.

Sssss.

Sorry.

It's broke too, I guess.

I'll get us out of here by morning.

Christine lights another candle, heaves herself up, and crosses to the dresser, opening one drawer after another. In the top one she finds crayons, a small cloth pouch; in the middle one mice scat and the remnants of a child's underwear: socks, a slip, panties. She pulls out a pale yellow top and holds it up for Heed to see.

That's your bathing suit.

Was anybody ever this small?

Mine in there?

Don't see it. Christine wipes perspiration from her face and neck with the fabric, then tosses it on the floor. She moves back to Heed and seats herself with difficulty at her side. Candleflame lights their hands but not their faces.

Was you ever a whore?

Oh, please.

People said.

People lied. I never sold it. Swapped it, though.

Same as me.

No you didn't. You were too young to decide.

Not too young to want.

Well? Was he good to you, Heed? I mean really good?

At first. For a few years he was good to me. Mind you, at eleven I thought a box of candied popcorn was good treatment. He scrubbed my feet till the soles was like butter.

Damn.

So when things got bad I relied on May and you to explain it. And when that didn't work I blamed everything on when he started losing money. I never blamed him.

I always did.

You could afford to. The sheriff wasn't breathing down your neck.

I remember him. They fished together.

Fished. I'll say. He forgot what every pickaninny knows. Whites don't throw pennies in your cup if you ain't dancing.

You saying Buddy Silk broke him?

Not him; his son, Boss. He was friends so to speak with the father but the son was another breed of dog. He did better than break him. He let him break hisself.

How you mean?

A little loan here, a bigger one there. Went along and went along. He had to pay, you know, to stay open and sell liquor in the place. It was tight but okay. Then the old Silk died and the new one upped the fees. We couldn't pay the bands, the police, and the liquor man too.

How'd you manage for so long?

Luck. I found some fishing pictures.

Heed gives Christine a look.

No.

Oh, yeah.

Who? Where?

Who cares who? And "where" was the bunk, the deck, the pilot's chair, anyplace and anything on board. Make you think twice about what a fishing rod can catch.

Men have the shortest memories. They always want pictures.

Huh.

Heed sighed, picturing Boss Silk. Herself standing there, afraid, wavering from damp sweat to chill. Wondering if he wanted sex or just her humiliation; or maybe the money he'd come for plus a quick feel. Shame he wanted, for sure, but she didn't know if it included her tits. In any case, she had been sold once and that was enough. "Here's something he wanted you to have." She handed him a brown envelope and hoped he would think it was money. Then turned her back to let him open it in private and to convey her own ignorance about men's business. When she heard him remove the contents, she said, "By the way there's another envelope used to be around here somewhere. But it was addressed to your mother care of the *Harbor Journal*. If I find it, should I give it to her or mail it to them? Want some iced tea, suh?"

Heed recounts the meeting in mammy accent with bulging mammy eyes. They chuckle.

Did he? Have a set for the old lady?

I made that part up.

Hey, Celestial.

Aw, girl. When did we first start that?

Playing at the beach one day, when they were about ten years old, they heard a man call out "Hey, Celestial" to a young woman in a red sunback dress. His voice had humor in it, a kind of private knowing along with a touch of envy. The woman didn't look around to see who called her. Her profile was etched against the seascape; her head held high. She turned instead to look at them. Her face was cut from cheek to ear. A fine scar like a pencil mark an eraser could turn into a flawless face. Her eyes locking theirs were cold and scary, until she winked at them, making their toes clench and curl with happiness. Later they asked May who she was, this Celestial. "Stay as far away from her as you can," May said. "Cross the road when you see her coming your way." They asked why and May answered, "Because there is nothing a sporting woman won't do."

Fascinated, they tried to imagine the things she does not hesitate to do regardless of danger. They named their playhouse after her. Celestial Palace. And from then on, to say "Amen," or acknowledge a particularly bold, smart, risky thing, they mimicked the male voice crying "Hey, Celestial."

Except for the words they had invented for secrets in a language they called "idagay," "Hey, Celestial" was their most private code. Idagay was for intimacy, gossip, telling jokes on grown-ups. Only once was it used to draw friendly blood.

Ou-yidagay a ave-slidagay! E-hidagay ought-bidagay ou-yidagay ith-widagay a ear's-yida-gay ent-ridagay an-didagay a andy-cidagay ar-bidagay!

Ave-slidagay. That hurt, Christine. Calling me a slave. Hurt bad.

It was meant to. I thought I would die.

Poor us.

What the hell was on his mind?

Search me.

When he died I said Bingo! Then right

away I took up with somebody exactly like him. Old, selfish, skirt-chasing.

You could have stayed here if that's what you wanted to be tied to. He had so many women I lost count.

Bother you?

Sure.

Did L know what was going on out on his boat?

Probably.

I meant to ask you. How did she die?

How you think? Cooking.

Frying chicken?

Uh-uh. Smothering pork chops.

Where?

Maceo's. Dropped dead at the stove.

She never came back after the funeral?

Nope. I thought you'd come back for hers. Didn't May write you?

She did, but I was in a fancy apartment banging my head over some rat.

The doctor?

Kenny Rio.

Traded?

Bought. Like a fifth of whiskey. And, well, you know, at some point you have to buy more. I lasted three years. Miss Cutty Sark.

You were nobody's liquor.

Neither were you.

What then?

A little girl. Trying to find a place when the streets don't go there.

L used to say that.

Jesus, I miss her.

Me too. Always have.

We could have been living our lives hand in hand instead of looking for Big Daddy everywhere.

He *was* everywhere. And nowhere.

We make him up?

He made himself up.

We must have helped.

Uh-uh. Only a devil could think him up.

One did.

Hey, Celestial.

Even in idagay they had never been able to share a certain twin shame. Each one thought the rot was hers alone. Now, sitting on the floor braving the body's treason, with everything and nothing to lose, they let the phrase take them back once again to a time when innocence did not exist because no one had dreamed up hell.

It is 1940 and they are going by themselves

to play at the beach. L has packed a picnic lunch for them and as always they will eat it in the shade and privacy of Celestial Palace: a keeled-over rowboat long abandoned to sea grass. They have cleaned it, furnished it, and named it. It contains a blanket, a driftwood table, two broken saucers, and emergency food: canned peaches, sardines, a jar of apple jelly, peanut butter, soda crackers. They are wearing bathing suits. Heed is wearing one of Christine's, blue with white piping. Christine's is a yellow two-piece; midriff, it is called. Their hair has been quartered into four braids so they have identical hairstyles. Christine's braids are slippery; Heed's are not. They are walking across the hotel lawn when one remembers that they have forgotten the jacks. Heed volunteers to get them while Christine waits in the gazebo and guards the food.

Heed runs into the service entrance and up the back stairs, excited by the picnic to come and the flavor of her bubble gum. Music is coming from the hotel bar—something so sweet and urgent Heed shakes her hips to the beat as she moves down the hallway. She bumps into her friend's grandfather. He looks at her. Embarrassed—did he see her wiggle her hips?—and in awe. He is the handsome giant who owns the hotel and who nobody sasses. Heed stops, unable to move or say "Excuse me. Sorry."

He speaks. "Where's the fire?"

She doesn't answer. Her tongue is trying to shift the bubble gum.

He speaks again. "You Johnson's girl?"

The reference to her father helps and her tongue loosens. "Yes, sir."

He nods. "What they call you?"

"Heed, sir." Then, "Heed the Night."

He smiles. "I should. I really should."

"Sir?"

"Nothing. Never mind."

He touches her chin, and then—casually, still smiling—her nipple, or rather the place under her swimsuit where a nipple will be if the circled dot on her chest ever changes. Heed stands there for what seems an hour but is less than the time it takes to blow a perfect bubble. He watches the pink ease from her mouth, then moves away still smiling. Heed bolts back down the stairs. The spot on her chest she didn't know she had is burning, tingling. When she reaches the door, she is panting as though she has run the length of the beach instead of a flight of stairs. May grabs her from behind and scolds her about running through the hotel. Orders Heed to help carry sacks of soiled bed linen through to the laundry. It takes only a minute or two, but May Cosey has things to tell her about public behavior. When she is finished telling Heed how happy they all are that she and Christine are friends and what that friendship can teach her, Heed runs to tell Christine what happened, what her grandfather did. But Christine is not in the gazebo. Heed finds her behind the hotel at the rain barrel. Christine has spilled something on her bathing suit that looks like puke. Her face is hard, flat. She looks sick, disgusted, and doesn't meet Heed's eyes. Heed can't speak, can't tell her friend what happened. She knows she has spoiled it all. In silence they go on their picnic. And although they fall into the routine—using made-up names, arranging the food—the game of jacks cannot be played because Heed doesn't have them. She tells Christine she could not find them. That first lie, of many to follow, is born because Heed thinks Christine knows what happened and it made her vomit. So there is something wrong with Heed. The old man saw it right away so all he had to do was touch her and it moved as he knew it would because the wrong was already there, waiting for a thumb to bring it to life. And she had started it—not him. The hip-wiggling came first— then him. Now Christine knows it's there too, and can't look at her because the wrong thing shows.

She does not know that Christine has left the gazebo to meet her friend at the service entrance. No one is there. Christine looks up toward the window of her own bedroom, where Heed would be looking for the jacks. The window is open; pale curtains lift through it. She opens her mouth to call out, "Heed! Come on!" But she doesn't because her grandfather is standing there, in her bedroom window, his trousers open, his wrist moving with the same speed L used to beat egg whites into unbelievable creaminess. He doesn't see Christine because his eyes are closed. Christine covers her laughing mouth, but yanks her hand away when her breakfast flows into her palm. She rushes to the rain barrel to rinse the sick from her yellow top, her hands, and her bare feet.

When Heed finds her, Christine doesn't explain the bathing suit, why she is wiping it, or why she can't look at Heed. She is ashamed of her grandfather and of herself. When she went to bed that night, his shadow had booked the room. She didn't have to glance at the window or see the curtains yield before a breeze to know that an old man's solitary pleasure lurked there. Like a guest with a long-held reservation arriving in your room at last, a guest you knew would stay.

It wasn't the arousals, not altogether un-pleasant, that the girls could not talk about. It was the other thing. The thing that made each believe, without knowing why, that this par-ticular shame was different and could not tol-erate speech—not even in the language they had invented for secrets.

Would the inside dirtiness leak?

Now, exhausted, drifting toward a maybe permanent sleep, they don't speak of the birth of sin. Idagay can't help them with that.

Heed needs more Stanback and coughs when she swallows it. A rasping cough that takes a long time to quiet.

Where does it hurt?

Name it.

Be light soon.

Then what?

I'll carry you.

Yeah, sure.

Hey! Look what I found.

Christine holds up the pouch and empties it, spilling five jacks and a rubber ball on the floor. She collects the five and fans them out. Too few for a game. She takes enough rings from her fingers to complete the set. Stars mixed with jewels sparkle in fresh candlelight.

Heed can't bounce the ball, but her fingers are perfect for scooping.

Hating you was the only thing my mother liked about me.

I heard it was two hundred dollars he gave my daddy, and a pocketbook for Mama.

But you wanted to, didn't you? Didn't you want to?

Quickly Christine scoops four, then groans. The thorn in her shoulder is traveling down her arm.

I wanted to be with you. Married to him, I thought I would be.

I wanted to go on your honeymoon.

Wish you had.

How was the sex?

Seemed like fun at the time. Couldn't tell. Nothing to compare it to.

Never?

Once.

Hey, Celestial.

I'd just as soon our picnics. 'Member?

Do I. We had Baby Ruths in the basket.

And lemonade.

No seeds, either. L spooned out the seeds.

Was that baloney or ham?

Ham, girl. L wouldn't go near baloney.

Did it rain? Seem to remember rain.

Fireflies. That's what I remember.

You wanted to bottle them.

You wouldn't let me.

The turtles scared us.

You're crying.

So are you.

Am I?

Uh-huh.

I can barely hear you.

Hold my . . . my hand.

He took all my childhood away from me, girl.

He took all of you away from me.

The sky, remember? When the sun went down?

Sand. It turned pale blue.

And the stars. Just a few at first.

Then so many they lit the whole fucking world.

Pretty. So so pretty.

Love. I really do.

Ush–hidagay. Ush–hidagay.

In unlit places without streetlamps or yelping neon, night is profound and often comes as ease. Relief from looking out for and away from. Thieves need the night in order to be furtive, but can't enjoy it. Mothers wait for it yet are braced all through their sleeping. The main ingredient offered by the night is escape from watching and watchers. Like stars free to make their own history and not care about another one; or like diamonds unburdened, released into handsome rock.

No one answers when he calls out, "Anybody here?" Guided by the weak beam of a flashlight, Romen crosses the lobby and climbs the stairs. It will be daylight soon, but now everything is hidden. He hears a light snoring to his left through a half-open door. He pushes it wide and dapples the beam over two women. He comes closer. Both look asleep but only one is breathing. One is lying on her back, left arm akimbo; the other has wrapped the right arm of the dead one around her own neck and is snoring into the other's shoulder. As he pours light into her face, she stirs, focuses, and says, "You're late," as though they had an appointment. As though stealing the car was not an impulse but an errand she had assigned him. As though what Junior told him hadn't mattered.

He had been asleep and woke up thinking about getting something to eat when she told him.

"You left them there?"

"Why not? . . . Turn out the light, sugarboy."

Romen was reaching to turn off the lamp but found himself scooping up the car keys instead. He got up then and dressed. Whatever Junior was saying, shouting, he couldn't decipher. He ran—fast, down the stairs, out the door, chased by the whisper of an old man. "You not helpless, Romen. Don't ever think that." Stupid! Clown! He was trying to warn him, make him listen, tell him that the old Romen, the sniveling one who couldn't help untying shoelaces from an unwilling girl's wrist, was hipper than the one who couldn't help flinging a willing girl around an attic. He backed out of the driveway and sped into the road. Slower, he thought. Slower. The road has no shoulders. Ditches beckoned on either side. One headlight blinked and died.

Junior huddled over her knees holding them together in her arms. Rocking back and forth, she was remembering how Romen had raised her foot from the bathwater and tasted it as though it were a lollipop. It was when they left the tub, both wet and clean as gristle, that the slipperiness had begun. A kind of inside slide, that made her feel giddy and pretty at the same time. The solid protection she'd felt the first

night in the house gave way to a jittery brightness that pleased and frightened her. Lying on
her back, she had closed her eyes to study it.
Finally she turned to look at Romen's face.
Deep in postcoital sleep, his lips parted, his
breathing light, he did not stir. This beautiful
boy on whom she had feasted as though he
were all the birthday banquets she'd never
had. The jitter intensified and suddenly she
knew its name. Brand-new, completely alien, it
invaded her, making her feel wide open and
whole, already approved and confirmed by the
lollipop lick. That was why, later on, when he'd
asked her a second time, she told him the
truth. Clearly, just the facts. His response, "You
left them there?", surprised her as did his sudden rush to be gone. Reaching to turn out the
lamp, he'd grabbed the car keys instead, and
got dressed as fast as a fireman. She called his
name, then shouted: "What? What?" He didn't
answer. He ran.

Junior left Heed's bed and roamed the
house. She didn't want to see the Good Man
or sniff out his aftershave. He had been missing
for days now, and had not appeared in the
hotel attic or returned to his room. Con-
fronting his portrait, eager to report her clev-
erness in the hotel, she had suppressed
suspicions of his betrayal, and when Romen

arrived, she forgot about him. Then the lollipop was tasted, and the Good Man vanished
from his painting altogether, leaving her giddy
and alone with Romen. Who ran. Away from
her. As fast as he could.

Confused, she paced the rooms for a while,
ending up in the kitchen. There she opened
the oven and, squatting down, tore pieces of
crust from the blackened leg of lamb. Raven-
ously she jammed them into her mouth. But
the jittery brightness, less than an hour old, did
not fade. Not then.

Romen has to carry them both. One at a time,
one at a time down the stairs. Tucking the dead
one into the wide backseat; helping the other
one into the front.

"She gone?"

"No, ma'am. She's at the house."

She won't let him go to the hospital, insist-
ing he drive to Monarch Street. When they
arrive, light is finally breaking. The windows
are glazed peach; the house inhales the damp
air, its siding juicy with moisture. Romen car-
ries her down the steps into the kitchen.
Before he can seat her, Junior rushes in—big-
eyed, apprehensive.

"Oooo I'm so glad. I tried to get help and couldn't find anybody, then Romen came by and I made him go out there right away. You all right?"

"Alive."

"I'll make some coffee, should I? Where is . . . ?"

"Get in there and shut the door." Leaning heavily, her arm bent in Romen's, a hand clutching the back of a chair, she nods toward L's old rooms.

Junior looks at Romen. He looks back expecting to see pleading. There is none, only startle in her eyes, no fear or questioning. Holding her gaze without a blink, Romen watched the startle become calculation become a frown directed at the floor. Something was draining from her.

"Go on!"

Without looking up, Junior turns, goes into the room, and shuts the door.

"Lock it," she tells Romen. "The key is in the bread box."

He helps her into the chair, locks the door, then hands her the key.

"You got to take her to the mortuary. Find a phone and get an ambulance out here. Make haste."

Romen turns to leave.

"Wait," she says. "Thank you, Romen. Everything left in me thanks you."

"Yes, ma'am," he says, and heads for the door.

"Wait," she says again. "Take a blanket. She might get cold."

Alone, seated at the table, she speaks to the friend of her life waiting to be driven to the morgue.

What do we do with her?

A bullet sounds about right.

You okay?

Middling. You?

Hazy.

It'll pass.

I bet she's figuring out a way to get out before the ambulance comes.

No she's not. Trust me.

Well, she'll start yelling in a minute. Think she's shamed?

Ought to be.

Romen returns with a blanket. "I'll be right back," he says. "Don't you worry," he says, and opens the door.

"Step on it," she says, stroking the key with her thumb.

Should we let her go, little rudderless, homeless thing?

We could let her stay, under certain circum-
stances.

What difference would it make?

To me? None. Do *you* want her around?

What for? I got you.

She knows how to make trouble.

So do we.

Hey, Celestial.

Romen is speeding down Monarch Street,
trying as best he can not to disturb his passenger. He is serene, in control now, although
when he approached the car and looked back
at the house, unfriendly-looking clouds were
sailing over the roof of One Monarch Street,
their big-headed profiles darkening all save
one window, which, like the eye of a deter-
mined flirt, keeps its peachy glint.

*I see you. You and your invisible friend, inseparable
on the beach. You both are sitting on a red blanket
eating ice cream, say, with a silver coffee spoon, say,
when a real girl appears sloshing the wavelets. I can
see you, too, walking the shore in a man's undershirt
instead of a dress, listening to the friend nobody sees
but you. Intent on words only you can hear when a
real voice says Hi, want some? Unnecessary now, the
secret friends disappear in favor of flesh and bone.*

It's like that when children fall for one another.

On the spot, without introduction. Grown-ups don't pay it much attention because they can't imagine anything more majestic to a child than their own selves, and so confuse dependence with reverence. Parents can be lax or strict, timid or confident, it doesn't matter. Whether they are handing out goodies and, scared by tears, say yes to any whim, or whether they spend their days making sure the child is correct and corrected—whatever kind they are, their place is secondary to a child's first chosen love. If such children find each other before they know their own sex, or which one of them is starving, which well fed; before they know color from no color, kin from stranger, then they have found a mix of surrender and mutiny they can never live without. Heed and Christine found such a one.

Most people have never felt a passion that strong, that early. If so, they remember it with a smile, dismiss it as a crush that shriveled in time and on time. It's hard to think of it any other way when real life shows up with its list of other people, its swarm of other thoughts. If your name is the subject of First Corinthians, chapter 13, it's natural to make it your business. You never know who or when it will hit or if it can stay the road. One thing is true—it bears watching, if you can stand to look at it. Heed and Christine were the kind of children who can't take back love, or park it. When that's the case, separation cuts to the bone. And if the breakup is plundered, too, squeezed for a glimpse of blood, shed for the child's own good, then it can ruin a mind. And if, on top of that, they are made to hate each other, it can kill a life way before it tries to live. I blame May for the hate she put in them, but I have to fault Mr. Cosey for the theft.

I wonder what he would make of Junior. He was adept, you know, at spotting needy, wild women. But this is now—not then. No telling what this modern breed of junior woman is capable of. Disgraceful. Maybe a caring hand, a constant eye, is enough, unless it's too late and their sleep is merely a waiting, a smoldering, like a cinder in a mattress. One no sugar in the world can put out. Mr. Cosey would know. You could call him a good bad man, or a bad good man. Depends on what you hold dear—the what or the why. I tend to mix them. Whenever I see his righteous face correcting Heed, his extinguished eyes gazing at Christine, I think Dark won out. Then I hear the laugh, remember his tenderness cradling Julia in the sea; his wide wallet, his hand roughing his son's hair . . . I don't care what you think. He didn't have an S stitched on his shirt and he didn't own a pitchfork. He was an ordinary man ripped, like the rest of us, by wrath and love.

I had to stop him. Had to.

Just as well they fought over my menu, looking in it for a sign of preference and misreading it when they did. Heed's grasp of handwriting skills was lim-

ited, but she had to wonder in 1971 if the "sweet Cosey child" her husband was willing property to in 1958 was neither her nor Christine but a baby on the way. They never saw the real thing—witnessed by me, notarized by Buddy Silk's wife—leaving everything to Celestial. Everything. Everything. Except a boat he left to Sandler Gibbons. It wasn't right. If I had been allowed to read what I signed in 1964 when the sheriff threatened to close him down, when little children called him names and whole streets were on fire, I might have been able to stop him then—in a nice way—keep him from leaving all we had worked for to the one person who would have given it away rather than live in it or near it; would have blown it up rather than let it stand as a reminder of why she was not permitted to mount its steps but was the real sport of a fishing boat. Regardless of what his heart said, it wasn't right. If I had read it in 1964 instead of 1971, I would have known that what looked like seven years of self-pity and remorse was really vengeance, and that his hatred of the women in his house had no level. First they disappointed him, then they defied him, then they turned his home into a barrel of quarreling she-crabs and his life's work into a cautionary lesson in black history. He didn't understand: a dream is just a nightmare with lipstick. Whether what he believed was true or no, I wasn't going to let him put his family out in the street. May was sixty-one; what was she supposed to do? Spend her old age in a straitjacket? And Heed was almost forty-one. Was she supposed to go back to a family who had not spoken to her since Truman? And Christine—whatever she was into wasn't going to last. There wasn't but one solution. Foxglove can be quick, if you know what you're doing, and doesn't hurt all that long. He wasn't fit to think, and at eighty-one he wasn't going to get better. It took nerve, and long before the undertaker knocked on the door, I tore that malicious thing up. My menu worked just fine. Gave them a reason to stay connected and maybe figure out how precious the tongue is. If properly used, it can save you from the attention of Police-heads hunting desperate women and hardheaded, misraised children. It's hard to do but I know at least one woman who did. Who stood right under their wide hats, their dripping beards, and scared them off with a word—or was it a note?

Her scar has disappeared. I sit near her once in a while out at the cemetery. We are the only two who visit him. She is offended by the words on his tombstone and, legs crossed, perches on its top so the folds of her red dress hide the insult: "Ideal Husband. Perfect Father." Other than that, she seems content. I like it when she sings to him. One of those downhome, raunchy songs that used to corrupt everybody on the dance floor. "Come on back, baby. Now I understand. Come back, baby. Take me by the hand." Either she doesn't know about me or has for-given me for my solution, because she doesn't mind at all if I sit a little ways off, listening. But once in a while her voice is so full of longing for him, I can't help it. I want something back. Something just for me. So I join in. And hum.

LP

12/03

MOR   Morrison, Toni.

Love.

LARGE PRINT

3000

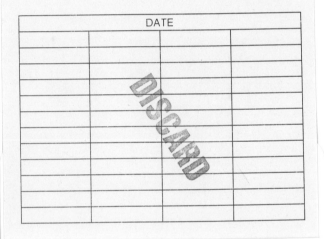

DATE		